Cinderella

(as if you didn't already know the story)

by
barbara
ensor

A YEARLING BOOK

This is a work of fiction. Names, characters, places, and incidents either are the product of the author's imagination or are used fictitiously. Any resemblance to actual persons, living or dead, events, or locales is entirely coincidental.

If somebody really does remind you of someone real, is that against the law?

 Published in the United States by Yearling, an imprint of Random House Children's Books, a division of Random House, Inc., New York. Originally published in hardcover in the United States by Schwartz & Wade Books, an imprint of Random House Children's Books, New York, in 2006.

Yearling and the jumping horse design are registered trademarks of Random House, Inc.

Visit us on the Web! www.randomhouse.com/kids

Educators and librarians, for a variety of teaching tools, visit us at www.randomhouse.com/teachers

The Library of Congress has cataloged the hardcover edition of this work as follows:
Ensor, Barbara.
Cinderella (as if you didn't already know the story) / by Barbara Ensor. – 1st ed.
p. cm.
Summary: In this updated version of the Cinderella story, Cinderella writes letters to her dead mother apologizing for not being more assertive, which she remedies soon after marrying the prince.
ISBN 978-0-375-83620-6 (trade) – ISBN 978-0-375-93620-3 (lib. bdg.)
ISBN 978-0-307-48295-2 (ebook)
[1. Fairy tales. 2. Folklore.] I. Title: Cinderella (as if you did not already know the story). II. Cinderella. English. III. Title.
PZ8.E596Ci 2006
[398.2]–dc22
2005012999

ISBN 978-0-375-87387-4 (pbk.)

Printed in the United States of America
10 9 8 7 6 5 4
First Yearling Edition 2011

ANNE SCHWARTZ AND
LEE WADE WAVED
MAGIC WANDS TO
MAKE THIS BOOK HAPPEN
THANKS TO DOVER
PUBLICATIONS
FOR
PICTURE
RESOURCES
SPECIAL THANKS
TO JULIETTE BORDA, BRITTANY
BURKE, DAVID COWAN, MADELINE
CRAVENS, KAROLINA ENSOR, T.
VALORIE FISHER, KAREN HATT,
DEXTER HOFFMAN, GEORGIA HOFFMAN,
MATT MITLER, BRIDGET ORR,
STEVE RICHARDSON &
MICHAEL RICHARDSON-WILSON
This story is based on a version of "Cinderella" written by Charles Perrault in 1697

For my father

Cinderella is what I am calling her from the beginning, even though I don't know what people actually called her back then. I'm definitely not just going to call her Charlene when for all I know her name was Naomi, because that's how rumors start. Like the one about the stepsisters being ugly, which is such a lie. The truth is, they were nice enough to look at, maybe not as pretty as you or Cinderella, but certainly not ugly. All right, some of what they *said* was ugly, yes, I agree, but we are getting ahead of ourselves now. Trust me, everything else in this story is one hundred percent true.

* * *

Cinderella was a little older than you when this whole thing started, a really nice girl. I'm sure the two of you would have liked each other. (Too bad you didn't know her then; Cinderella could so have used a friend like you.)

Now the actual story is about to begin.

"If anyone knows of any reason why this couple should not be joined in holy matrimony, let them speak now or forever hold their peace."

Nobody said anything out loud during the brief silence that hung over the room after the minister spoke those words. So the wedding ceremony for Cinderella's father and her new stepmother went ahead as planned. (In case you want to know if the children of one person not liking the children of the person they are marrying would be enough reason to call a wedding off, the answer is NO. Because in a strict legal sense only the adults are getting married.) Nothing else could be said or done after the minister told everyone the couple was now

Nice for *her,* Cinderella thought, but my dad was *already* a man.

Still, if this made her dad happy, it made Cinderella happy too. And all the guests thought she should be happy.

"You lucky girl!"

"I bet you're thrilled!"

Of course she was, and she was smiling at everyone so that there would be no doubt about it.

Cinderella did feel a little queasy, though. She hadn't been able to get to sleep the night before, and it didn't help that her real mother wasn't around to smooth the sheets and give her a cup of warm milk. Cinderella didn't love her stepmother yet, and she didn't love her new stepsisters either . . . but she decided that was perfectly okay.

"First you have to get to know them" was what her mother would have said, and it was true. What was also true, though, was that Cinderella didn't even think she *liked* them. A person couldn't help noticing,

they didn’t seem very friendly.

It made the edges of her smile hard to hold up.

Cinderella's mother was no longer alive. But for some reason Cinderella couldn't help worrying about what it would be like if her mother ran into the new stepmother as they were both heading to the bathroom in the middle of the night. Or if the two of them were trying to make coffee at the same time. It wouldn't be pretty.

After the ceremony Cinderella went back to her room, took off her stiff patent leather shoes,

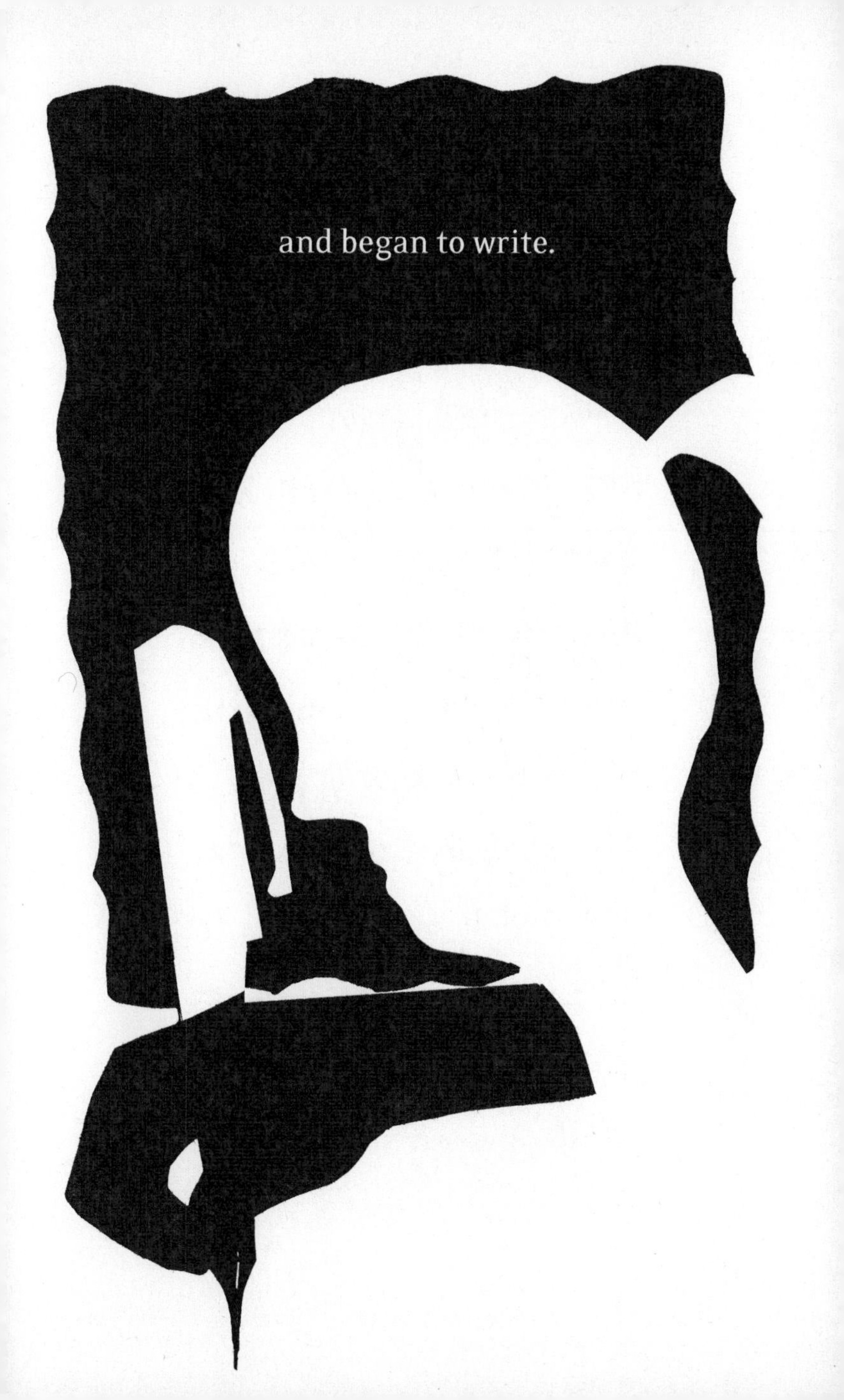
and began to write.

Dear Mama,

I regret to inform you that ~~Dad~~ your husband has married ~~again~~ a second time. ~~This is perfectly legal.~~ ~~It did seem a little soon.~~ I don't expect you will be able to read this, but in case you can I did want to be the one to tell you myself. ~~so you don't find out about it in an unpleasant way.~~

The lady has two daughters who are older than me. To be honest, and don't repeat this to anyone, they seem a little stuck-up.

I'm sure everything will work out fine—Dad says it will. I hope this isn't too much of a shock. ~~It's not going to be a real family like you and me and Dad~~.

They are moving a bunch of furniture pretty soon, so I gotta go.

Your Daughter 4 ever,

Cupcake

P.S. Does everyone always talk about how the bride looks? Do they mean she looks good in *comparison* to how she looks on other days? I don't get it. I guess I'll have to figure it out on my own.

P.P.S.

Don't worry about writing back,
I don't expect miracles
or anything.
(we don't believe in them,)
or do we?

The honey-colored wallpaper, candy pink curtains, and comfy furniture that Cinderella and her mother had picked out so carefully all made her stepmother shudder.

"So sweet!" her stepmother said, and managed to make it sound like an insult. Then she went out and hired a professional decorator to help her express what she called her "personal vision for the interior." Every picture of Cinderella's mother—except "Well, all right, just that one over the kitchen mantel"—had to go. And it wasn't "Dad's room" anymore; it was suddenly "our room." Already it smelled of her stepmother's icky perfume. Cinderella felt sorry for the house itself, which had a sadness about it now, like a tugboat forced to dress up as a yacht.

If you had visited Cinderella's house

a week after the wedding, you would hardly have recognized it. Sprawled on a four-poster bed, in what used to be Cinderella's room, her elder stepsister was complaining about "what a dump" they had moved into. Next door the second stepsister was telling a friend what a "weirdo" their new sibling was. On her way to her own room, Cinderella always tiptoed by their doors to give the girls a little privacy.

Cinderella's new room was at the very top of the house—where it got roasting hot in the summertime and you had to huddle under lots of blankets in the wintertime. The only place she could stand up straight was in the very center.

"My girls' furniture could not possibly fit up there," her stepmother had explained with a helpless little shrug.

Dear Mama,

As you might have noticed, I am sleeping in the attic now, where you didn't even think we should put the kittens! I have to admit I didn't say anything, but don't get mad. I knew my stepsisters would get the good rooms anyway, and they would turn all red in the face if I showed I minded. I thought maybe they would

begin to ~~love~~ like
me if I just moved
my stuff without
complaining.

Unfortunately,
that didn't exactly
work. If you were
here I ~~wou~~ bet you could
help me stand up to my new

Stepmother. But of course if you were here, I wouldn't need to (not that it's your fault or anything). I miss you a lot.

Bye 4 now,
Cupcake

P.S. Dad looks a little pale. He might be working too hard.

Cinderella didn't see much of her father anymore. When he was around he always seemed to be in a hurry to get to the office. He was an accountant. Now that he had married Cinderella's stepmother, he had decided to stop playing clarinet with the bebop band on Tuesday nights.

"I can't believe what you spent on that woman's funeral!" Cinderella's stepmother would often say as her father slipped out the back door in the morning. Cinderella was usually asleep when he got home, tired out from all her chores.

And there were always lots of chores. A long list would be waiting for Cinderella when she got home from school.

1. Sweep the stairs
2. Don't answer the door in your work clothes
3. Get rid of fingerprints on the light switches
4. Look a little cheerful
5. Do not hum
6. Clean the toilets
7. Don't complain to your father
8. Crumbs in the kitchen encourage mice, so clean up *immediately* after your sisters

It all had to be finished before Cinderella went to bed. If her stepmother didn't like the way something was done, she would throw a conniption fit.

"Didn't your mother teach you anything?"

Sometimes it seemed as though the more Cinderella tried to make her stepmother happy, the more angry her stepmother became. When that happened, Cinderella would imagine the skin on her face stretched out flat—like a balloon that was too full of air. This made it easier for Cinderella to look like she was paying attention when her stepmother spoke, without being stung by her cruel words.

After mopping the floor one Saturday morning, Cinderella settled onto the wooden chair by the fireplace. From where she sat, she and her mother's picture could see each other pretty well. Cinderella was just about to tell her mom about the tomatoes that were almost ready to pick in her vegetable garden when her stepsisters burst noisily into the room. Cinderella could tell they were in one of their giddy giggly moods.

(Now, remember, I told you before, nobody called her Cinderella yet.)

Just the sight of their earnest little stepsister, wearing dirty hand-me-downs and gazing at the burnt-out cinders from last night's fire, struck the two of them as hilariously funny. "Cin-der-ella!" the elder one said in a low singsong voice, and they both howled with laughter.

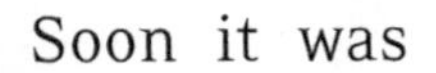
Soon it was

"Cinderella, have you
cleaned my room yet?"

"Cinderella, my shoes
need to be sorted by color."

And even her stepmother would call out,

"Cinderella,
my dress needs
ironing–right now!"

or

Cinderella was her name.

The poor girl seemed to be running up and down stairs all the time now. To the basement for a pair of gloves, to the attic to get the ironing board, to the kitchen to make a face pack, then up the stairs to the bathroom to start in with the curling iron. She couldn't seem to run fast enough. She would have done anything to make them like her—even just a tiny little bit—but nothing worked.

"What is *wrong* with you?"

Her stepsisters were impossible to please.

"So are you coming to the ball or what?" the elder stepsister asked Cinderella one day. Two pairs of eyes neatly outlined with eyeliner (with powdered lids and lashes loaded with mascara) looked intently at Cinderella.

"Ball?" asked Cinderella, taken aback.

"I didn't know there was going to be a ball."

"She thinks we like trying out new hairstyles every day of the week," the younger one giggled, nudging her sister.

"All three of us have been invited to

the prince's ball," the elder explained slowly, as if English were not Cinderella's native tongue.

"It's at the palace," the second stepsister added, patiently. "Everyone's going to be there. I mean, you know, not *everyone,* but . . ."

"Technically, you see," the elder continued, "the invitation is for you as well."

"Strictly speaking," added the younger one, to underline the theoretical nature of Cinderella's invitation.

It was not hard to see what her step-sisters wanted her to say.

Cinderella swallowed hard. "I think . . . I'd better not," she said.

"Got something more important going on that evening?" inquired the elder, catching her sister's eye.

"I don't have the right clothes, and it would be too . . . weird," said Cinderella quickly, looking away, in case her eyes began to tear up.

"Suit yourself," her stepsisters said.

Obviously relieved, the two of them began clawing through rings and bracelets in their jewelry boxes.

The next morning, Cinderella wrote to her mother.

Dear Mama,

~~Please~~ Don't be mad at me. I know you are already. What fun would it be going to the ball with everyone wishing I wasn't there?

She tore the letter into tiny pieces without writing any more. She didn't like the feeling that her mom was looking over her shoulder disagreeing with every word she wrote.

The ball would be that very evening.

As her stepsisters surveyed themselves in the full-length mirror, Cinderella wound strands of their hair around a curling iron to make ringlets.

"Maybe the prince will pick one of you two for his bride–I would if I were he!" their mother said, poking her head around the door. "Then we could all get out of here and go live in the palace."

As she looked more closely, she spotted a speck of lint on the younger daughter's gown and angrily went to pick it off.

"If he doesn't marry one of you, we will all know who to blame!"

Dear Mama,

This might not interest you all that much, but I did want to stay in touch.

Here are some sketches of the dresses my stepsisters have pretty much decided to wear. I really hope they don't change their minds again. (Because I'd never be able to finish fixing up new ones in time and they'd get so mad.)

Anyway, I've got
to sew on
some
buttons,
better run.

Hope you are well, Cupcake

It's kind of hard to
get their hair
to stay up
like this.

"I bet our little stepsister wishes she were coming now," the younger sister said as she took a last look at herself in the mirror.

"Too late!" said the elder one triumphantly.

"You both look gorgeous.
Have a wonderful time."

Cinderella closed the door and sat down next to a pile of laundry to have a good cry.

"You wish you could go to the ball, don't you?" said a total stranger who was suddenly standing next to her.

Cinderella, too shocked to say anything, nodded mutely.

"I'm your fairy godmother," the lady said, as though this would clear up any confusion.

Cinderella could not wipe the startled look off her face.

"I don't know why you look so surprised," said her

godmother, starting to sound impatient.

Cinderella opened and closed her mouth a few times, but no words came out.

"We'll have you on your way in no time, Cupcake," her godmother continued breezily. "There are a few little errands your godmother needs you to help her with first. Could you get me that rather nice pumpkin I noticed out in the garden?"

After that the fairy's demands became more challenging. "Your mother used to have one of those thingamajigs," her godmother announced, pantomiming that she was a prisoner behind bars.

"Huh?" replied Cinderella.

"You know, for catching mice!"

Cinderella ran two steps at a time

down to the basement. Six mice had followed the smell of cheese into the trap. Now they were waiting to be let loose in the garden again, as per usual.

"Perfect!"

said her godmother when the metal box

full of rodents was set down in front of her.

"Now I need a really top-notch driver," she said, and she cast her eyes around the room. "Someone really trustworthy, who has a way with the horses."

"I'll check the rat trap," said Cinderella, surprised to hear the words coming out of her mouth.

"Terrific idea!" said her godmother, her eyes lighting up.

Cinderella came back with a particularly hideous fat old rat, which clearly delighted the fairy.

"Now stand back," she said importantly. A wave of her wand transformed the whiskered rat into a nattily attired driver for the coach. His whiskers became a mustache, carefully waxed to curve up like the handlebars on a bicycle. His pointy nose poked out eagerly from under a top hat. His girth took on an air of distinction beneath an expertly tailored suit. Already the former rat was enthusiastically cracking a whip.

"Do hold your horses, Charles!" Cinderella's godmother scolded him gently. There were no horses yet, and Charles the coachman looked suitably embarrassed.

Like a child joyfully waving a sparkler, the fairy godmother crisscrossed her wand, and the sturdy orange pumpkin exploded into an elegant gold coach supported by delicate wheels. The sumptuous interior was upholstered in a tartan plaid. A gentle tap on the head of each gray mouse produced a group of startled horses. The coachman patted each of the dappled team in a way that settled them down immediately. They were ready to go anywhere.

Cinderella could not believe her fairy godmother was going to all this trouble for her. She was about to tell her it wasn't necessary when her godmother barked another order. "Be a good girl and get me, um . . ."

She bit her lip, looking to see what was missing. "Some nice-looking lizards, I saw some in your garden. . . ."

While her godmother was still trying to remember exactly where it was she had seen them . . . six lizards that had been sunning themselves on a flat rock were abruptly awakened. Cinderella reached for them one by one. With their tails clasped gently between her thumb and forefinger, she presented them to her fairy godmother.

"Oh yessss!" said the godmother, delighted with the wriggly mass. A rhythmic motion of the wand turned them into six silk-clad coachmen chatting about last night's football game. The former lizards clung effortlessly to the decorative doodads all over the coach.

"And now it's your turn, my dear. My goodness, you are as lovely as your mother." Her godmother's wand traced

circles around Cinderella, who instantly began to change.

chapter 5

There was a whooshing sound, then a pop like a cork being pulled out of a champagne bottle, and then Cinderella let out a little scream. The person in the mirror hardly even looked familiar. Some spark of beauty, scarcely visible to the naked eye before, had become a blazing fire. A new dress, simple, floaty, and elegant, was almost part of her. Gorgeous ivory-colored

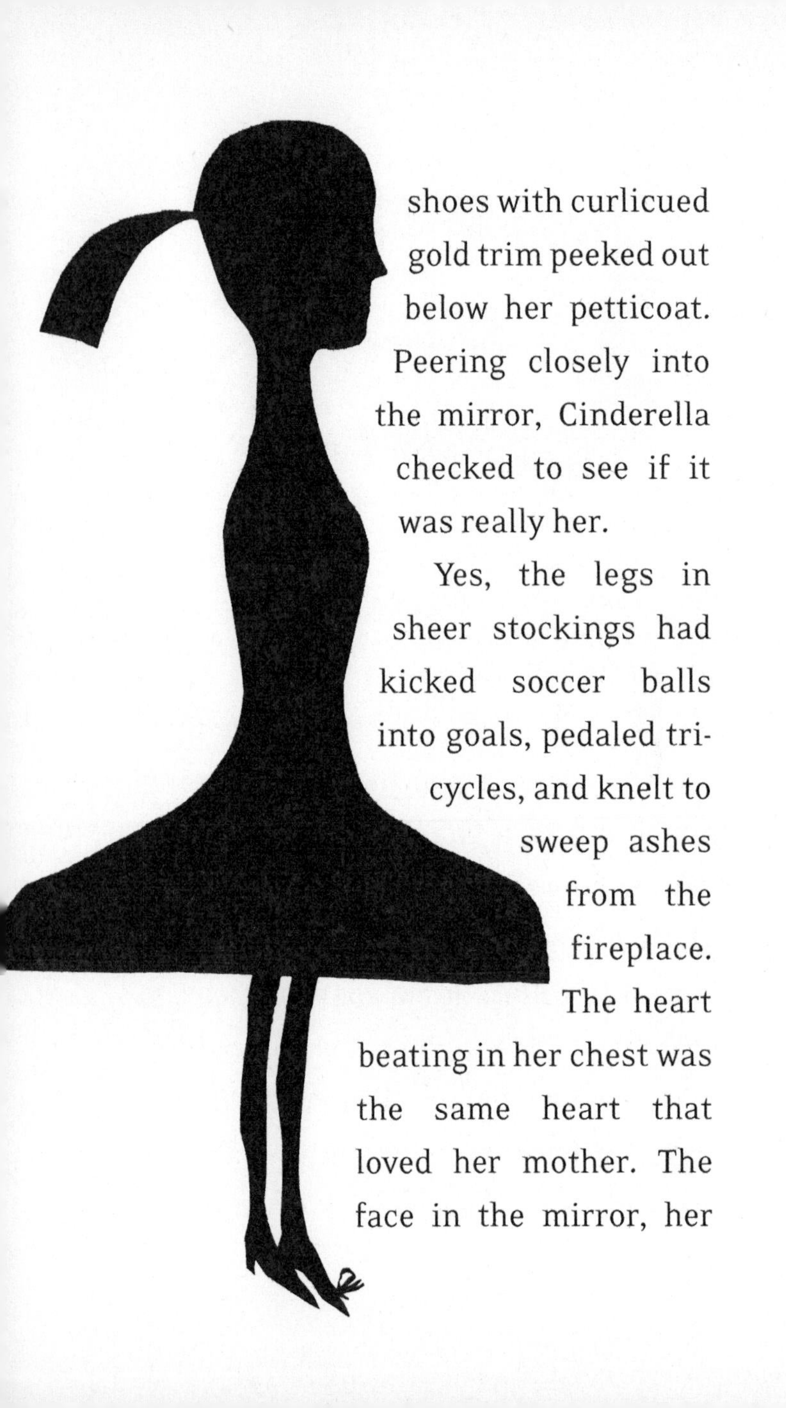

shoes with curlicued gold trim peeked out below her petticoat. Peering closely into the mirror, Cinderella checked to see if it was really her.

Yes, the legs in sheer stockings had kicked soccer balls into goals, pedaled tricycles, and knelt to sweep ashes from the fireplace. The heart beating in her chest was the same heart that loved her mother. The face in the mirror, her face, was flushed with excitement. Cinderella gave herself a little hug.

Her fairy godmother told the driver not to go too fast. Then, turning to Cinderella, she said sternly, "You need to be home by midnight, dear. That's part of the package. *Midnight,* do you hear me?

"And by the way, dear, do you like the shoes?"

Cinderella nodded that she did. She was still trying to take it all in. She had woken up a girl that morning. Now she was something else, a butterfly released from its chrysalis. For a moment, she thought about running back

to her room and locking the door. She wanted to get under the blankets and write a letter to her mother.

Then she took a deep breath. She saw

that the driver and horses were restless to trot into the night air. Cinderella knew that she was ready too.

"I don't know how to thank you

enough," she said to her godmother.

"Thank me by being back by mid-night!"

Midnight is hours from now. Why

does she keep harping on about mid-night? Cinderella wondered. I'll probably want to leave a long time before that.

"Midnight, or there's going to be a very serious consequence!" her fairy godmother shouted, running alongside the carriage as it clip-clopped away.

"Definitely by midnight," Cinderella called back.

From inside the carriage Cinderella noticed that she lit up the landscape around her. If she smiled, everyone on the street looked happy. If she frowned, so did they.

As the carriage slowed to a stop outside the palace gates, one of the lizards—now a coachman—offered his arm to steady Cinderella down the carriage steps.

chapter 6

The massive palace door groaned open, and Cinderella glimpsed a world as orderly and well mannered as a clock. Impeccably dressed couples danced tidy minuets on elaborately patterned floors.

But with Cinderella's entrance into the ballroom, everything stopped. The threads of conversations snapped, violin strings stopped vibrating, and even loud colors fell silent. Not a medal or a monocle glistened, not an ostrich feather wavered.

"I say, darling, who is that lovely?"

"Let me look through my opera glasses, Bubsy.

Oh, look at that. It *is* a princess,

you can *always* spot them."

There was a gasp as anyone standing near a column leaned against it for strength.

Half the guests whispered, "Who is that?"

The other half shook their heads and gestured that they didn't know.

Above the gold chandeliers, the opulent hors d'oeuvres, the fringed curtains, and the potted palms stood the king and queen, looking down on it all. Up there in that exalted world of cloud-painted ceilings and operatic arias, their crowns had begun to weigh heavily on their heads. You could see it in the lopsided way they smiled at each other.

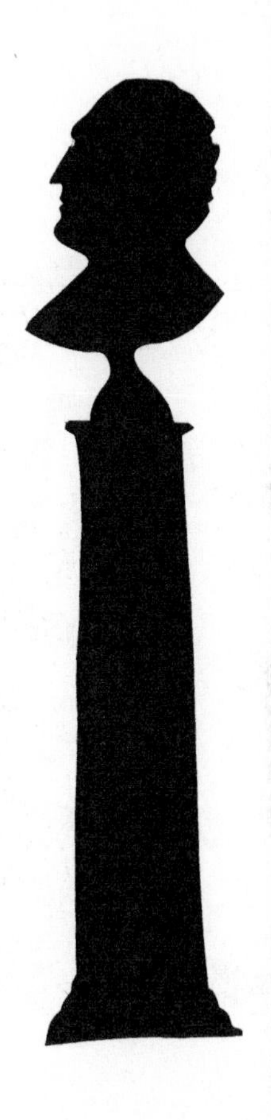

Spellbound, the impeccably dressed couples watched as the prince walked

all the way across the giant room

to ask Cinderella with an eloquent gesture if she would care to dance.

"I'd be delighted, Your Highness."

Where had she learned to speak as royally as that? Cinderella wondered.

And so Cinderella and the prince danced as though they had always known each other. People's necks

lengthened, their jokes became funnier, and the tuba player improvised a melodious solo. The laughter, clinking of glasses, straightening of bow ties, and beckoning of waiters became bigger, livelier, and louder.

The couple danced and danced, circumventing Doric columns, dodging

waiters with silver trays. It was only when they stopped dancing that things got awkward.

"Let's get some air," said the prince.

"All right," replied Cinderella.

They stepped out onto the balcony and into the moonlight. She looked marvelous, he told her. Well, his dancing was sublime, she told him.

With nothing left to say, they returned to the ballroom and let the saxophones and violins speak for them.

For the rest of the evening, the music carried them wherever it wanted. They never did get around to exchanging names and phone numbers.

Thanks to years of dance instruction, the prince expertly fox-trotted Cinderella over to a red-carpeted part of the room, cordoned off by a velvet rope. A royal mountain of filet mignon and cubes of quivering Jell-O in jewel-like colors awaited. A general was carving some steak. A royal waiter balanced glasses of champagne on a silver tray. Two cousins of the prince helped themselves from dessert tables piled high with whipped cream, studded with imperial berries, and flecked with colored sprinkles.

"All my favorite foods," the prince explained, loudly enough to be heard over the music, as they helped themselves to a little bit of everything.

"Why no yellow sprinkles?" Cinderella mouthed back.

"I don't like those as much, so they take them out," said the prince.

"Oh," Cinderella replied, and her mouth stayed in a circle.

When Cinderella looked over her shoulder to see what all the commotion was about, she was surprised to see her two stepsisters at the center of it all. Their hair had stayed up nicely, she noticed with satisfaction. The two of them were loudly lambasting a man in tights who was guarding the velvet rope.

"It isn't exactly fair. . . ."

"The food looks better in there, and it's carpeted. . . ."

"I am so very sorry," the man in tights told them stiffly. "This section is strictly for the cream of the crop, their close friends, and hangers-on."

"Are you calling us hoi polloi?"

"Suggesting we are riffraff?"

"*Mesdemoiselles*, you must understand I am here to follow the wishes of the king and queen."

It didn't seem fair to Cinderella either. Why should she be on one side while her own stepsisters were stuck on the other? Without thinking, she scooped up two chocolates wrapped in gold and handed them to her stepsisters as consolation. The prince, glancing up from his filet mignon, was touched by Cinderella's generosity.

Suddenly, Cinderella felt a pang of worry. Might the sight of their stepsister lolling about in the red-carpeted zone instead of doing laundry back home bring on a fresh round of indignation? She froze momentarily at the thought. But it was obvious by the way the girls blushed and curtsied that they did not recognize her.

Her head was in the clouds, and she could tell the prince's was too. She had almost forgotten the other world where she used to live. None of that seemed real

anymore. Then she heard the clock begin to chime and looked to see what time it was.

⁂

"Yikes!" Cinderella gasped, her royal syntax falling away.

The prince was too busy helping a blob of emerald green Jell-O onto a spoon to notice her dashing out. Neither did anyone else as they moonwalked and lollygagged across the floor.

As Cinderella ran across the ballroom, her left shoe fell off.

By the massive door she felt herself grow lighter and swifter. Her gown had vanished, and she was back in her old clothes again. Outside, she noticed a rat lumbering off into the shadows and several smaller creatures scuttling away. A solitary pumpkin sat by the side of the road. Cinderella took off the remaining shoe, tucked it into her pocket, and ran barefoot all the way home.

"I guess I got my consequence," she thought.

Cinderella went straight up to her room. Turning on the little lamp by her bed, she began to try to make sense of what had happened.

Dear Mama,

If you were still here I might not want to talk to you about this, because you would ~~probably~~ laugh and maybe tell all your friends. But, I guess, well, here goes: I think I might really be in love. I mean for real. That's the good part. The strange part is that it is with this prince, who I don't even know (apart from what his favorite foods are). I can tell he loves me back, which

should also be a good part. But
he thinks I am someone else
who I'm really not, which is just
terrible. I'll explain that in a minute.
I guess I'll never even see him again,

which is ~~absolutely~~ the
part I can't believe.
I still feel airborne.
This is going to make
doing chores again feel like
a real thud. ~~But~~ Okay,
now let me back up
a bit....

Cinderella wrote several pages explaining in great detail how her fairy godmother had appeared out of nowhere and turned useless stuff around the house into everything she had needed to go to the ball. When she was done she could imagine the look on her mother's face, so she added,

p.s. Listen, I know it's asking a lot to expect you to believe ~~all~~ any of what I've written here. Just think about the fact that you are reading this letter—that's pretty strange too. So you see, you never know.

Underneath she drew a funny picture of a person looking surprised, with her mouth open and her hair standing on end.

chapter 8

Meanwhile, back at the ball, one of the prince's servants brought him the little shoe left on the floor. The mystery girl had gone

without

even saying

goodbye!

Mournfully carrying the shoe on a small velvet pillow, he asked the servants who stood near the doors if any of them had seen a lady with just one shoe leaving in a bit of a hurry.

None of them had.

The prince felt happy and sad at the same time—happy to have found the girl of his dreams, sad to have lost her. His stomach lurched as if he were on a roller coaster. The mystery girl was so gloriously different from his mother, he thought, as he watched the queen waddle off to her bedchamber. His mother was a stickler for introductions; she would *never* go without saying goodbye. He laughed out loud at the idea of his mother leaving a shoe behind.

The prince took a quick inventory. He was happier than he had ever been. He was sadder than he had ever been. Nobody had ever ditched him or enchanted him like this.

He could never marry anyone else. He would like to marry her. All of which meant he needed urgently to find her. Right away, whatever her name was.

—•—

While the prince was pining for her, Cinderella heard voices outside her

window and pretended to be fast asleep. Stomping loudly up to her room, her stepsisters had a lot to say. "You were such an idiot not to come," began the elder.

"You should kick yourself!" suggested the younger.

Cinderella tried to look suitably distressed. Next her stepsisters proudly displayed the chocolates–the ones she herself had given them earlier.

"Look, but don't touch!" said the elder.

"Did someone *give* them to you?" asked Cinderella slowly, trying to sound curious.

"Not just *someone*!" scoffed the elder.

"How can we even explain it to her?" lamented the younger sister.

"Girls!"

Their mother shouted up the stairway.

He needed to find the mysterious girl. By the next morning the prince had begun to pace. What else could he do besides walk around in circles? His very life hung in the balance, he thought. It was all so desperately glorious and gloriously desperate.

It shocked the prince to see how alone he was. His parents, who until recently had seemed such reasonable creatures, wanted to know why the whole business couldn't be discussed over dinner after a civilized game of golf.

"Golf–during a national crisis?" The prince could hardly believe his ears.

It had begun to occur to the prince that his parents were a lot less wise and witty than he had once thought. Their jokes, for example, were not really all that funny. People laughed so loudly because they were the king and queen. Now the awful knowledge that his parents were actually a couple of complete imbeciles crashed down on the prince's head. As he watched them lumber off with their golf clubs, it was suddenly obvious: he would have to handle this all by himself.

The prince summoned the royal advisors.

"The person who fits this shoe will be my wife," he told them, holding up the dainty shoe on a velvet pillow.

"All sorts of other people
might fit that particular
shoe, Your Highness. . . ."

"A boy, and not a girl, could easily . . ."

"Judging from the size of it,
the person might still be in
elementary school . . ."

". . . which could have all . . ."

The prince was exasperated by their ridiculous drivel.

"I guess I'll just have to look for her by myself," he declared.

The prince asked two servants to have his finest horse saddled. He put on a full suit of armor and wielded a mighty sword. A little flag would add a nice touch, he decided. The prince himself carefully bore the tiny shoe on the small velvet cushion. The servants came along to help with map reading, bugle blowing, and knocking on doors.

Because Cinderella had seemed so at home fox-trotting past portraits of his

titled ancestors, the prince felt sure she was well-to-do.

"She must live up one of these long driveways, or perhaps in a gated community," the prince told his servants as they started on their quest.

Word of the princely expedition had spread, and girls from hoity-toity families thrust their feet delicately out of windows to save His Highness the mortification of speaking with their own particular mothers and fathers.

Alas, every female foot in the high-end neighborhoods proved too big for the tiny shoe. Now the prince pictured a lonely life ahead of him—devoted to writing love poetry with a quill pen.

"Such a brief moment of happiness," he despaired, "and now an eternity of sorrow."

In these moods the prince could be a royal pain. So as they knocked on doors of the non-hoity-toity, his servants did their best to humor him.

"Perhaps it is she, and not her family, who is noble," the first suggested.

The thought had never occurred to the prince, and he knew immediately that his servant was right.

"You should be proud of this brave undertaking whatever the outcome," said the other, and the prince realized he was. Very proud. These two short men were wiser than all his royal advisors and his parents put together. He had been so right to leave home and head out like this on his own . . . almost.

No one else in his family had done anything half this hard, or risky, or romantic, he thought. He pictured how good he must look wearing his armor, glinting in the sunlight, with the flag fluttering in the breeze. If he couldn't respect his parents anymore, at least he could look up to himself. The thought cheered him.

Startled by a loud rap on the door, followed by a noisy bugle salute, Cinderella's stepmother strode angrily forward.

"Who is it now?" she shouted. She had already forgotten what came next on the list of chores she was writing out for Cinderella.

She opened the door a crack, and the sight of the prince at the bottom of the garden path, resplendent in a full suit of armor, turned her scowl into a fawning smile.

"His Royal Highness the prince asks that all unmarried ladies in this house try on this particular shoe," announced one of the servants, waving an impossibly small ivory and gold shoe on a little velvet pillow.

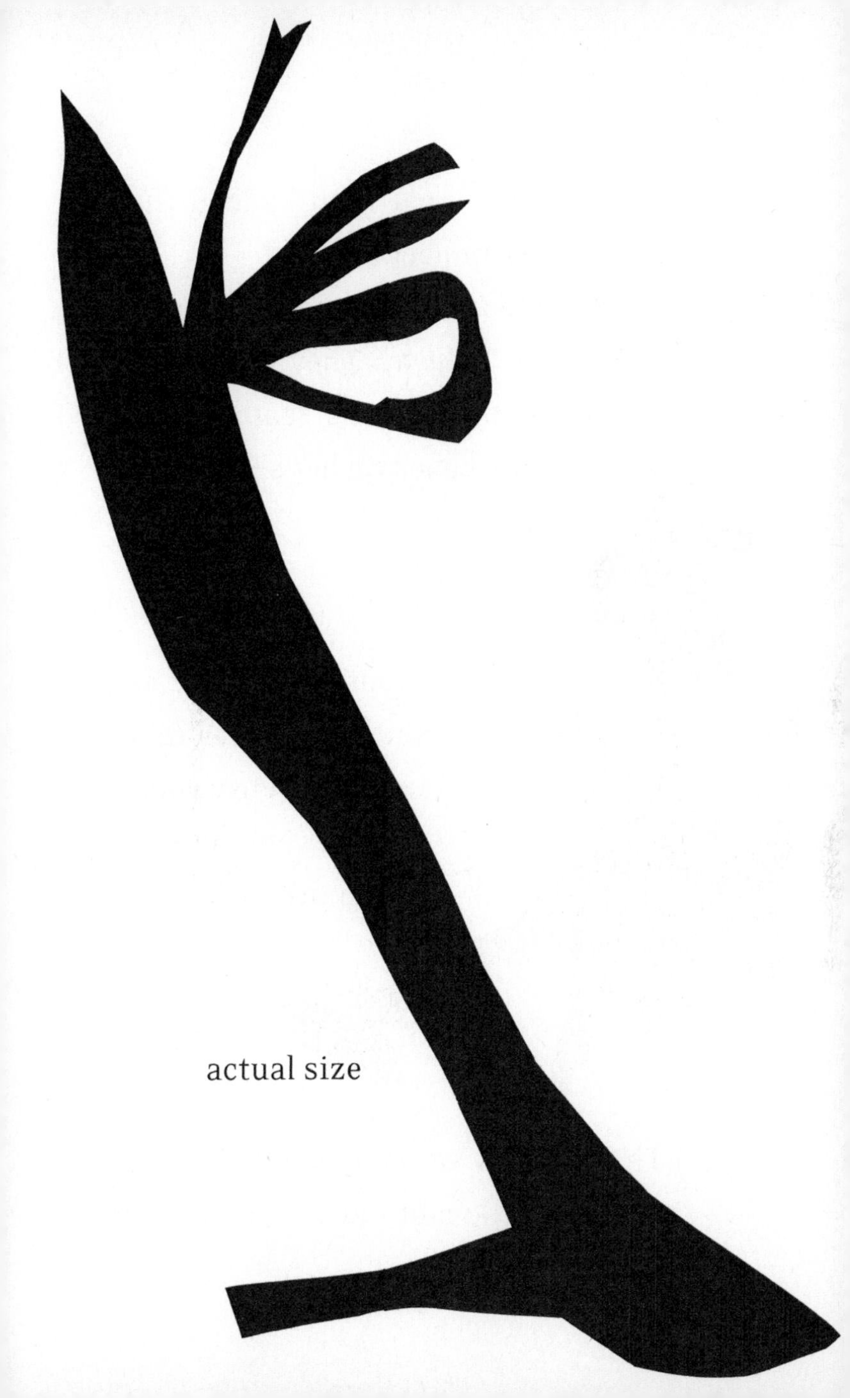

actual size

"It is his personal wish," added the other servant, importantly.

The two stepsisters skidded to a stop in the front hallway. They had heard about the prince's search for a wife based on her shoe size.

"It fits!"

shouted the elder as she stuffed her foot into the teensy shoe, her heel poking way out in the back.

The prince's servant could see she was lying, so he motioned to her sister to try on the shoe. Her feet were even bigger, so the second sister suggested,

"If it would please His Highness, I would be willing to undergo the ordeal of foot reduction surgery."

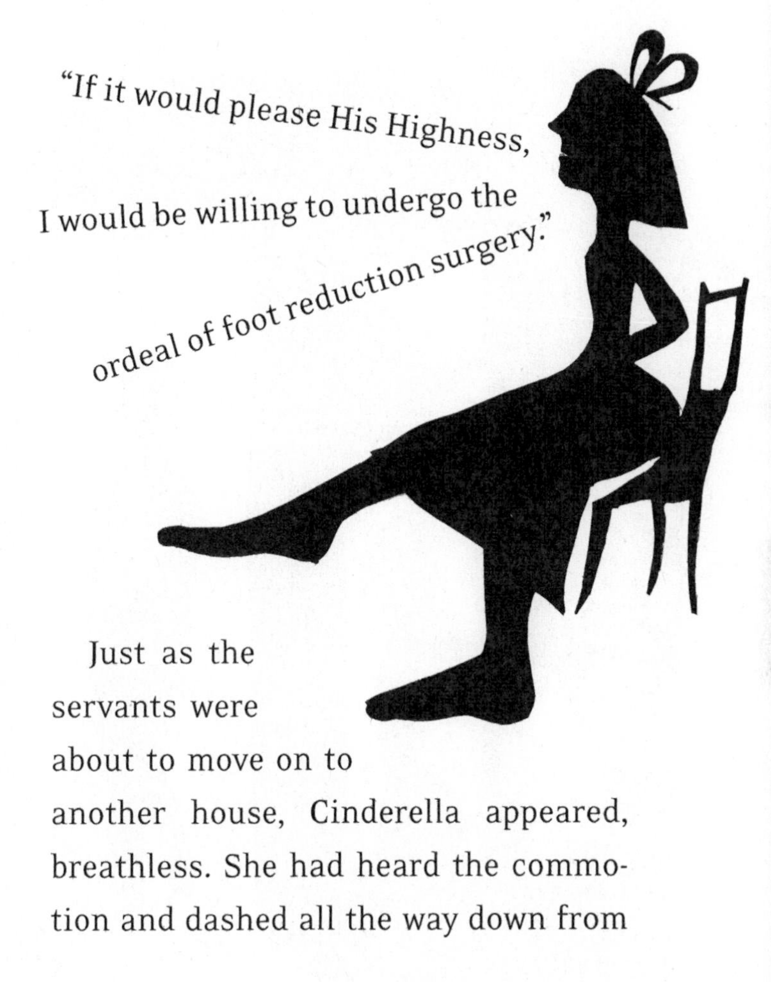

Just as the servants were about to move on to another house, Cinderella appeared, breathless. She had heard the commotion and dashed all the way down from

her room in the attic to see if there was something she could do to help.

Smiling at the lost ivory and gold shoe as if at an old friend, she slipped it on. Then she pulled its mate out of her pocket and put that shoe on her other foot.

At the end of the garden path, the prince was beside himself with joy. He had found her at last!

As quickly as he could in a full suit of armor, the prince dismounted his horse and dashed up the pathway. It touched him to see that, like

him, his beloved was surrounded by idiotic family members. The two of them had so much in common, the prince thought, fighting back the tears.

As he drew near, the prince saw that the girl he had danced with looked even more adorable in her regular clothes. He loved her more now–even though he wouldn't have thought that was possible. He felt so awkward encased in armor. He wished it weren't so hard to move. . . . He wished . . . he knew her name.

Shyly, the prince whispered to one of his servants to inquire what the girl's name might be.

"Cinderella," Cinderella said happily, hearing the question.

At that the prince nervously dropped to one knee. His armor scraped noisily into its new position and made a clanking noise.

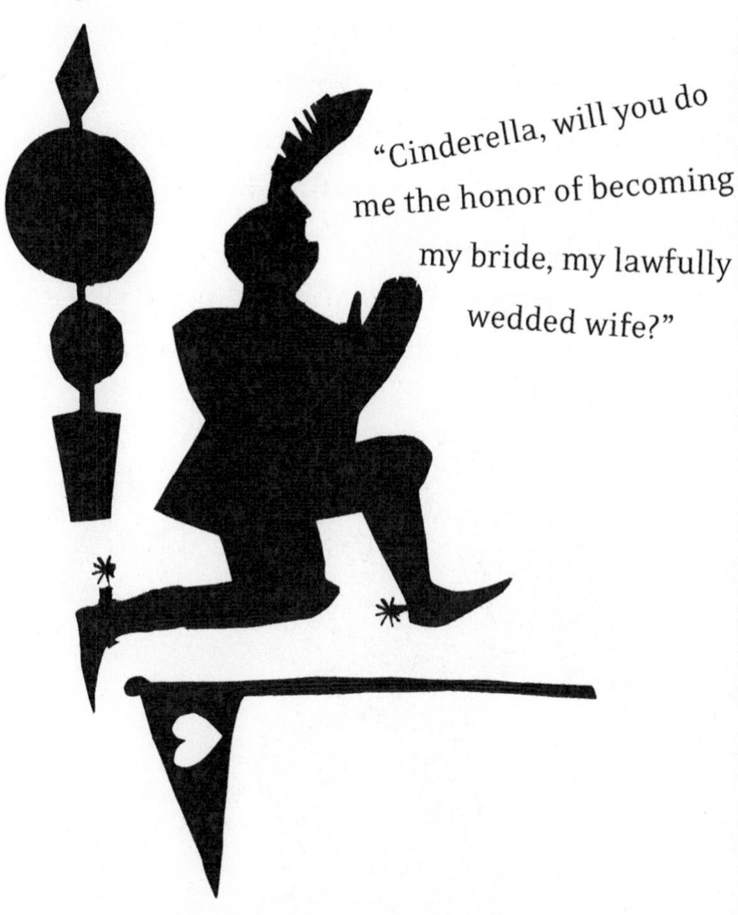

"Cinderella, will you do me the honor of becoming my bride, my lawfully wedded wife?"

His fate was in her hands now.

As Cinderella's jaw dropped in amazement, a whole ripple of events took place. First her fairy godmother appeared out of nowhere. An expert wave of her wand turned Cinderella back into the dazzling beauty of the night before.

Then her stepsisters, who could see that it was their own Cinderella who

had danced with the prince, began to sob.

"Please, please forgive us! We didn't know it was you!"

"We had no idea!"

Before she could even consider the royal proposal, Cinderella knew she had to get the noise to stop. She begged her stepsisters to quit boohooing. She helped them wipe the mascara off their cheeks.

Then Cinderella turned her attention to the prince. He looked terrible. It had been a full minute since he had asked for her hand in marriage and he was forgetting to breathe.

"Hmmmmmm," Cinderella said. Should she marry the prince? She just wasn't sure. She didn't really even *know* the guy, apart from, well, his favorite foods. He certainly was a good dancer . . . but then again. . . . Cinderella's heart beat loudly in her chest.

chapter 10

At last the answer came to her.

"Yes," said Cinderella, smiling radiantly.

"Yes!" she said again.

The prince hugged her and told her how overjoyed he was. Then he thanked the two servants who had accompanied him on his royal quest. Then he said he would never take anything for granted for the rest of his life. Then the fairy

godmother and the stepsisters and Cinderella's father and even her stepmother needed to wipe their faces with handkerchiefs

because they were so happy
it made them weep.

Usually this is when the curtain flops down with the words

But there is more, of course, and I don't see why you shouldn't hear it.

As days became weeks, and weeks became months, Cinderella and the prince discovered that they were actually as different as a tree and a lake. It was hard sometimes, but it opened up a big landscape of possibilities for both of them. As the love between them grew, they began to trust themselves, even the dark scary places.

Dear Mama,

So much has happened with the peace treaties and the trade agreements lately, I hardly know where to begin.

The most important thing, though, is I think the prince loves me just the way I am even when I make mistakes.

Thank you, Mama, for everything always.

Your Cupcake

The prince was no longer afraid of his own emotions; in fact, he wallowed in them. As king now, he sang songs–songs about his soppiest, saddest, most heartfelt feelings. They were songs that made people bring out their handkerchiefs to dab their tears away.

Cinderella was no longer a pushover. Her toughness as a diplomat brought a period of peace. With no wars, her husband's suit of armor was no longer needed, and it became a curious object that people stared at in a glass case in a museum.

"We want wildness!" Queen Cinderella told her astonished subjects in her new strong voice. "The best rooms in the kingdom will become places where birds can heal their broken wings and tired bats can rest." She and the king had already moved out of the palace into more modest accommodations.

"But your stepmother and I are very old now," Queen Cinderella's father begged.

"Oh, all right, you may stay on in that big house, provided you clean up after the pigs."

Her stepmother thanked Queen Cinderella for her generosity and swore she would sweep and mop night and day.

Queen Cinderella's stepsisters begged to be allowed to stay on as well. They desperately needed all that closet space for their fancy clothes, they explained.

"Desperately."

"Horribly."

"Not a chance," the queen's messenger told them. "The animals are moving in tomorrow."

So you see, nowadays, Queen Cinderella isn't afraid of anyone or anything. Nobody is her boss.

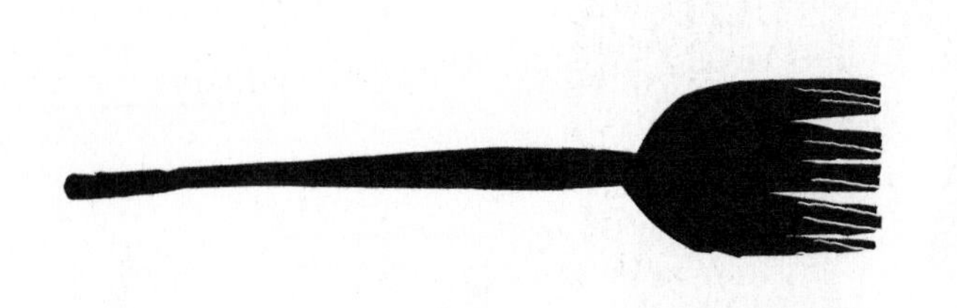

YOU ALREADY KNEW THIS STORY

NO MATTER WHERE IN THE WORLD YOU GREW UP OR WHEN YOU LIVED.

IN CHINA THE FAIRY GODMOTHER

IS A DEAD FISH WHICH USED TO BE HER PET.

HER MOM DOESN'T DIE IN INDIA. ~~INSTEAD~~ SHE GETS TURNED INTO A GOAT. IN DENMARK MOM IS STUCK BEING A COW.

SHE GOT TOO CLOSE TO THE FIRE, THE ALGONQUINS SAY, WHICH IS WHY HER HAIR CAUGHT ON FIRE AND HER FACE GOT ALL SCARRED ~~LIKE THAT~~.

IN ZIMBABWE IT'S A MAGIC SNAKE THAT HELPS HER. SOMETIMES THERE IS NO BALL. A HAWK JUST TAKES ONE SHOE DIRECTLY TO THE PRINCE.

GERMANS SAY THINGS END BADLY FOR THE STEPSISTERS: THEY GET THEIR EYES PECKED OUT BY BIRDS.

EVERY TIME A RAINBOW DIES

ALSO BY

RITA WILLIAMS-GARCIA

BLUE TIGHTS

FAST TALK ON A SLOW TRACK

LIKE SISTERS ON THE HOMEFRONT

RITA WILLIAMS-GARCIA

EVERY TIME A RAINBOW DIES

HARPERCOLLINS*PUBLISHERS*

The author would like to acknowledge
Ann-Marie Young for her assistance with this novel.

 For information address HarperCollins Children's Books, a division of HarperCollins Publishers, 1350 Avenue of the Americas, New York, NY 10019.
www.harperchildrens.com

Library of Congress Cataloging-in-Publication Data
Williams-Garcia, Rita.
Every time a rainbow dies / Rita Williams-Garcia.
p. cm.
Summary: After seeing a girl raped and becoming obsessed with her, sixteen-year-old Thulani finds motivation to move beyond his interest in his pigeons and his grief over his mother's death.
ISBN 0-688-16245-2 (trade) — ISBN 0-06-029202-4 (library)
[1. Caribbean Americans—Fiction. 2. Interpersonal relations—Fiction. 3. Rape—Fiction. 4. Brothers—Fiction. 5. Pigeons—Fiction. 6. New York (N.Y.)—Fiction. I. Title.
PZ7.W6713 Ev 2001 00-38900
[Fic]—dc21 CIP
AC

Book design by Alison Donalty
1 3 5 7 9 10 8 6 4 2
❖
First Edition

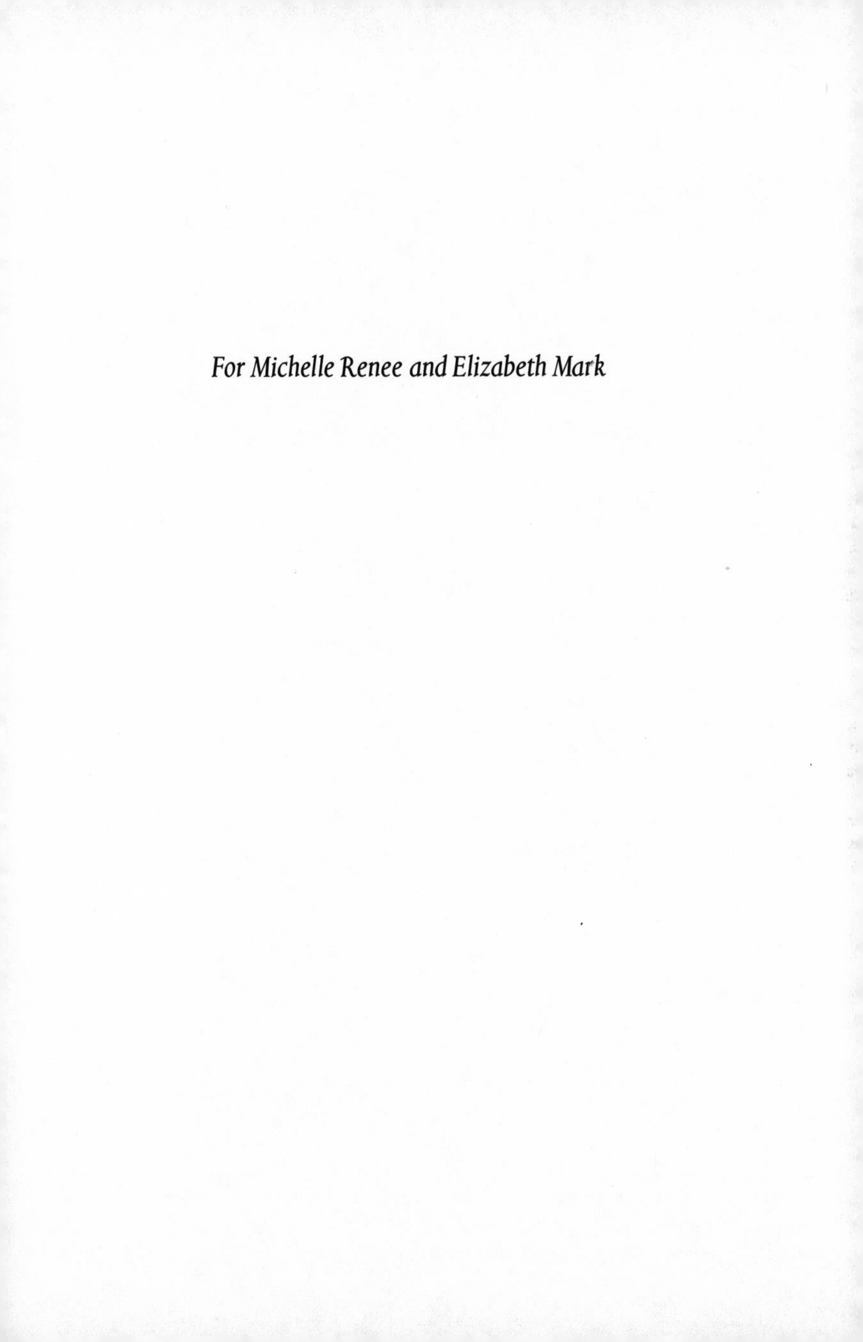

For Michelle Renee and Elizabeth Mark

EVERY TIME A RAINBOW DIES

ONE

From on top of Brooklyn, Thulani watched the sun bed the clouds, waiting, as he always did, for his birds to return. He woke each morning with one thought: freeing his birds. Their cooing pulled him from sleep, called him up the attic steps and onto the roof of his brownstone. Each and every time it gave him a thrill to unlatch the door of the dovecote he had built and find himself besieged by fourteen pigeons, each a variation of white: snowy, spotted, dingy, or wing-stained. Every morning without fail he dropped cereal or seeds on the asphalt roof, recalled the meanderings of dreams better told to birds than people, then watched them fly off toward Prospect Park. As sure as he knew the view from the rooftop, he knew his birds would always return to him.

Thulani looked out into the graying predusk. Below him, in their apartment, his sister-in-law, Shakira, rubbed her belly, waiting for her husband to come in from work. On the street city buses became scarce, leaving Eastern Parkway to gypsy cabs and vans. Store owners locked up their shops, and street vendors packed up their tables. The day was coming to a close.

Thulani gazed down upon a couple who stopped to kiss. He watched how the man held the woman's head with both hands as she pulled herself into him. Even if they had felt his eyes, they would not have cared. From above them he could see that the world around the two did not exist.

Caught up in this couple, their kiss, and thinking about what drew people to be entwined so, Thulani was suddenly surprised by a legion of wings flapping about him.

One by one, five rock doves descended on him, their pink feet touching down on his arms and shoulders; the nine other birds stopped at his feet.

Of his birds, he loved Yoli and Dija best, two of three snowy hens he found as squabs on his roof. Yoli was the first to recognize him as a "mother," and Dija followed her lead. Their sister, Esme, however, was indifferent to his attention. Of all his birds, she would be the one to run off with another flock.

His treasured cocks, Bruno and Tai-Chi, were brothers with identical black wing stains whom Thulani could easily tell apart. Bruno was bold, a leader, and Tai-Chi, the graceful one, was proud of his wingspan. Both birds had become his when they followed Esme to the rooftop one evening, but they had eventually mated with her sisters.

These were the only birds he had bothered to name. The three hens, the cocks, and their brood were simply "my birds." Truer friends did not exist. In the two years since Thulani had become owner and caretaker of his flock, there had been no discord, no change in routine, and, in spite of Esme's iffiness, no defections. His birds needed him to free them in the morning; he needed them to return before nightfall. Only when they died would they leave him.

In an act of dominance Bruno hopped from Thulani's shoulder to his head. Thulani grabbed Bruno's feet and carefully pried the bird's talons from his dreadlocks. "Stop showing off for Yoli. I know she's yours."

He threw Bruno up to the sky, then flung the others perched on his arms airborne as well. This was how his birds began their chasing game—running, hopping, and flying in circles around the roof. Each bird aimed for Thulani, to land on his shoulders, arms, or head.

Bruno wanted his head, but Thulani swerved, missing

those pink feet. He twisted, turned, waved his arms, and ducked. He could not shake Bruno or Tai-Chi, nor could he resist his hens.

When he tired or they tired, or when Shakira yelled up from the apartment window, "Cut the mischief!" he unlatched the door of the dovecote so they could roost.

"Home," he said in response to their cooing and flapping. "Home."

On his word they gathered to be let into the dovecote, an improvement on the avocado crate from Yong Moon's Fresh Fruits. The crate had served Yoli, Dija, and Esme as squabs but would not do as the three sisters grew into voluptuous hens that attracted other birds to the rooftop. In shop class he had made a bigger home with a lock and a swinging door. He had enjoyed building the dovecote and was at ease with a hammer.

"Home, Dija; home, Yoli; home, Bruno," he coaxed, until all hopped into the dovecote to roost.

Only one hen, Esme, lingered. Esme refused to breed, which went against the very nature of a hen. He'd watch his cocks do the mating dance, puff their necks, bob their heads in and out, and hop to one side, only to be spurned by Esme, who took the role of coquette too far, never allowing any to catch her. Even though Esme had attracted many male pigeons, a mourning dove, and a seagull, Yoli and Dija were responsible for increasing the brood.

"Home, Esme."

The lone hen stood her ground.

Thulani made kissing noises at her. This wouldn't do. He knelt and held out his hand filled with seeds, which caused a stir in the dovecote. Still, Esme showed no interest. She preferred to roost under the ledge where she and her sisters had been found, although the dovecote was kept clean and the water bowls were filled.

"Don't make me come and get you."

Esme tried to hop away. Thulani seized her, his thumb firmly planted against her beating heart. He grabbed her body before her wings could open. "It's better when you cooperate," he said, and dropped her into the box, then flipped the latch.

The July air began to cool. Thulani sat on the tarred roof next to his birds, his baggy T-shirt pulled over raised knees. Each pair, Yoli and Bruno, Dija and Tai-Chi, and others settled wing to wing. Even Esme recovered from the indignation of having been handled and joined in the low cooing.

"I *will* build a bigger home," he told his brood. "I will, I will, I will."

Lulled by the calm of murmuring birds, Thulani stayed on his roof well past midnight on summer nights like this. It was his refuge from Truman and Shakira and their desire to "man him up" for all his sixteen years. Here on his roof he had the waning sun, a cooling breeze, his birds, and eventually, when night pulled down, a place to lay his head. Now that his birds had cooed themselves to sleep, he put on his earphones to pipe in the old-style reggae his mother used to blast and his father once sang. With this music, the pattern of stars, the peace within him, he closed his eyes and hung in the summer cool. Only then could he indulge himself in a dream where his head lay in the lap of a girl he did not know, just to smell her, feel the scratch of her long nails against his neck and chest, look into her eyes.

During the time he dreamed of her, he learned what he could not do. He could not fix on her face too strongly, for she would turn into other things. He could not imagine them elsewhere, say, in his bed, for the bed would smother them, or at school, for she would be swallowed by the crowd. She and he could be together only on his roof, his head in her lap as her nails drew patterns over his body. As long as he knew this, she would stay with him and he would have a place to rest his—

A scream.

Where from?

His dream girl fled. His eyes popped open, and his hand flew up against the dovecote. He removed the earphones and set aside the cassette player. Was it a cat trying to get at his birds? No. A cat couldn't climb up to the roof. And the scream was human.

He checked his birds. They were shaken, but more so from his hand banging the cage.

"It's okay, it's okay."

There. Again. The scream.

Thulani was now on his feet, crouching low. He crept to the edge of the roof and looked down in the direction of the alley. In the dark he could see the Dumpster. Three figures were on the ground, eclipsed but not completely hidden by the Dumpster. He moved to the far right side to get a better angle. He saw them, out in the open, across the street in the alley. One guy, his pants down to his ankles, was on top of a woman. The other guy knelt by her head, holding her down while the first guy pumped her with his body.

Thulani stayed low, crouching and watching. When the one on top struck her, Thulani flinched to avoid the blow.

Move. Do something.

Vans passed by. A woman who had to have seen crossed the street.

Do something. *Something.*

The guy stopped pumping her. The other guy repositioned himself, maybe to hold her down better. Then the one on top, doing it, raised his arm and punched her in the face.

Thulani sprang tall. *"Hey, you!"*

The two guys stood and looked to the roof.

Thulani left his birds and The Wailers. He ran through the roof door, down the attic steps in a leap, down two flights of steps—"THULANI!"—past the blob that was his sister-in-law, and out in the street in a matter of seconds, his heart bursting through his chest. They had a knife to slice him up, a gun to shoot him full of lead. What did he have? One hundred and forty pounds of almost man, heart thumping through his chest, lungs pressing against his ribs.

He shot down the block, across the street, and into the alley. Die or be beaten, he had to do what he could for her.

His heart and lungs oozed out of his ears, but he was ready to face them. When he got there, to his relief the two had fled. He was alone in the alley, except for her.

He approached her carefully. She was alive but not fully conscious. He could also see that she wasn't a woman, but a girl, like any girl he'd go to school with.

They had left her with her legs still open and no clothes on, except for ripped panties at her ankles. Her top, bright and pink with skinny straps, had been torn from her body. Her plum-colored nipples were sticking out. Her vagina, a crushed rose, was fully exposed, its petals dripping blood. Her face had been messed up. One eye was swollen shut, and her lip was busted.

Although he had been with her for only ten or fifteen seconds, it seemed longer. He didn't know what to do next. Should he leave her? Get help? Cover her? What? What?

Finally he knelt over the girl, realizing he'd have to touch her.

Maybe she felt him breathing. He was breathing awfully hard. She stirred, although her eyes remained closed. When he tried to touch her shoulder, to let her know he was there, she thrashed about like something wild, discovering the power of her legs.

"I'm not them! I'm not them! They're gone," he said, tolerating her open palm slaps. "They're gone."

This would not calm her. Still with eyes shut, she reached out for a piece of him, just to hit him.

"I'm not them!" he repeated loudly. Finally her arms died in the air, and her legs lost their power. "Look, girl. I live right there. My sister-in-law can tend to you."

"No-no-noooo!" She flung her arms in the direction of his voice. Her eyes were still closed.

Had she come out of the house like this? A top and no clothes?

He took off his oversize T-shirt, a shirt he wouldn't let Shakira borrow.

The girl was in no shape to help herself. He would have to touch her, sit her up, put the shirt on her, if she'd let him. Or if he could get past her bruises, her gashes, her blood, her belly, her titties. He wanted to turn away, but he could not avert his eyes.

She struggled to raise herself. He lifted her into a sitting position, shoulders first. As he anticipated, she fought him. He did his best to slip the T-shirt over her head and guide her arms into the holes, while she wrenched her torso and spun her arms out and cursed him.

He had held frightened squabs but had never handled anything as delicate as this girl. He wanted to be gentle as he helped her to her feet, but she fought everything he did for her.

He didn't know what to do with her panties. One side was ripped completely. She could not bend to pull them up. When he tried to pull them up over her thighs, she screamed at him in words he didn't understand. He let them drop to the ground.

Her legs were weak. One foot turned in, and both legs shook. He knew that she would fall with her first step and that she would hit him if he tried to help her.

He grabbed her arm anyway. She slapped his hand, as he knew she would.

He refused to let go.

"I know you're hurting, girl, but don't hit me. Don't hit me. I'm not them."

She took two steps, then paused. He reached out to give her balance. She hit him again, in spite of what he had told her. What could he do but bear her blows?

When they reached the end of the block, she stopped, then leaned into him, allowing him to support her. She opened her one good eye as best she could and looked around.

"Where you live? I'll take you."

"No. I'm fine." Her accent was thick. "I can go."

"Can't leave you, girl."

Since she wasn't talking, all he could do was let her guide them at her pace, taking ten minutes to complete each city block. Anyone still on stoops stared as they passed. He saw heads behind shaded windows, and he wondered what they thought with their mouths and eyes wide open.

When they turned on Franklin Avenue, the girl kept saying, "Okay, okay." He figured they were near her house. She turned to him and said sharply, "Now, go!" and pushed him away.

He wouldn't leave her alone and said, "You go in first; then I'll go." Before she could protest, the door opened. A woman too old to be her mother stood in the crack of the door before opening it wide. She snatched the girl inside, screamed in what he thought was Creole, and slammed the door.

He feared for the girl. He stood and waited for a sign that she would be all right.

The scolding ended with a slap. Then another. He pressed himself to the door. The girl was sobbing and trying to explain. He had to get her out of there. Take her to the hospital, the police, or his house. He had to do something. He banged on the door.

"Girl? Girl, you all right in there?"

There was no answer.

Thulani was set to charge through the door when it swung open. The old woman came at him, yelling obscenities and waving his T-shirt as if it were a torch. He backed away, and she threw it at his chest.

The girl's voice pleaded in words he did not understand. She was telling the woman that he was not one of them.

It didn't matter. The old woman, still brandishing her fist, only knew what she saw. He with his filthy clothes on the girl's beaten-down body. Blood on her face, down her legs. He standing before her as if he had a right to be there.

Thulani backed away until he was running, in which direction it didn't matter. To the heads that looked out of windows, and to those who ventured outside to catch the action, he was guilty.

TWO

Thulani walked fast. Then he ran, down blocks, across avenues, even if they took him farther away from Eastern Parkway. Away from his house. His rooftop. His birds. He simply ran, stopping twice to mop his face, around his eyes with the T-shirt, the one the old woman had thrown at him, the one he had struggled to put on the raped girl's body. It didn't help. Wiping would not stop the pictures that played before him. Running could not put any bit of it behind him. Everywhere he turned masks followed him, vivid and distorted. He ran and ran but couldn't shake those sounds, those pictures. The scream, birds fluttering, the punch, one guy on top of her, the other holding her down, another punch—he still ducked—blood streaming from a busted lip, a closed eye, purple and swollen, plum-colored nipples, opened legs, the crushed rose, more blood, arms whirling, hands slapping, mad-crazy eyes of the old woman.

When he thought he would scream or lose his mind, he heard his mother's voice say, "Still yourself."

Thulani slowed to a trot, then a brisk walk, and none too soon. Up ahead he made out the distinct crawl of a blue-and-white in the next block. Spending his days on his rooftop did not make him ignorant of the streets below. He had seen enough to know how to carry himself and was determined to pass without being stopped by cops looking for a suspect.

The patrol car broke left on Nostrand. Thulani slid his hands in his pockets and tried to walk casually in case he was being watched. This was not easy, as he felt he looked guilty to anyone who saw him. Especially to the girl who would not stop hitting him, the old woman who cursed him in her language, and to the eyes that peeped out from behind curtains. Guilty.

She had to know that he had watched. That he could have been there thirty seconds sooner. That maybe she hadn't had to take that last punch. Her eye wouldn't be swollen, her lip busted up. She wouldn't have had to take so much from them if he had come down off the roof at her first scream. Why else would she continue to hit him when he told her to stop?

He was exhausted but not ready to come home. Home was where he settled, and he was far from doing that. He took President Street, which was still lively with people, then walked two blocks, where there was no one. When his head began to clear somewhat, and the images that haunted him were not as sharp, one thought occurred to him: They're still out there. They had to have seen him, even if it was dark.

Thulani turned into Kingston, then thought, What makes you think they're not on Kingston?

He turned down Bedford.

What makes you think they're not on Bedford? They could be packing. If they could rape her, they could just as easily shoot me.

Then he heard it again: "Still yourself."

Thulani turned up Prospect Place and told himself, What will be, will be. If he had to step to them, he would. He had no one to back him up besides his brother, Truman, and Thulani didn't carry anything to defend himself. For all the good it did him, he had fourteen birds on a rooftop and, to his surprise, some heart.

Thulani returned to his block on Eastern Parkway, back to everything familiar. Even so, he could not go inside his house. He was drawn to the alley and had to see the place where it happened. He looked down upon the spot where he had found her, knelt, and touched the rough ground where she had lain on her back. Though he could not see it, he knew her blood was on the street, perhaps where he ran his hand.

To look at it, a strip between a Chinese takeout place and a barbershop, there was no trace of a crime scene. Just a place from which you'd naturally turn your gaze. A place where men took a piss in broad daylight and sanitation workers collected garbage from the Dumpster in the early hours.

Even though he was not one to throw himself before people, he felt he should tell someone that a girl had been raped where he stood. But whom would he tell? Could he open his mouth and have sense come out? All through school teachers had implored him to speak up or speak clearly. Talking was not his favorite thing.

He stood up and dusted off the grit from his hands on his shorts. It was then that he saw some figure billowing up from the ground on the side of the Dumpster. He approached it carefully, for it seemed alive. Thulani grabbed the moving thing. His fingers discovered it was merely a piece of cloth.

The thin material slid through his fingers like silk, but it wasn't silk. It was a fine cotton. Almost sheer. He couldn't imagine why this fine cloth had been thrown away. When he held it up to the sky, he could see by the way the bottom danced in the breeze that it was a skirt.

Instantly he knew it was hers. He thought it was the kind of thing she would wear, though he did not know her at all. He pictured her wearing it.

He opened the skirt fully. It was a free-flowing skirt that was tied, not zippered or buttoned. The tie, a simple strip, had been ripped, yet managed to hang on to the body of the skirt by a few loose threads. He looked about. Someone could be watching him. He shook the street off the cloth and rolled it into a tight loaf that he held under his arm. It was time to go home.

Upon seeing him, Shakira, his sister-in-law, let out a gasp, an exaggerated one. "Ya look a sight!"

He shrugged but thought, Got to get past her.

Shakira did not mean to let him pass. She stood, her belly huge, and legs a big *A* before him. "And what do ya mean, chargin' through heah wild and crazy, scarin' poor Old Dunleavy to his grave?"

Mr. Dunleavy, a countryman from Thulani's mother's village, was the tenant in the first-floor apartment. He had been a retired photographer for many years when Thulani's mother rented to him ten years ago. His mother was fond of saying, "He knew me before my parents were born." Now Old Dunleavy was decrepit. Thulani laughed inwardly at Shakira's concern for their tenant. Both she and Truman had plans for that apartment as soon as the boneyard claimed Old Dunleavy.

"The food is put away. You'll have to fix your plate if ya want to eat."

Shakira waited for some reply, the usual thing he'd say about her half cooking. All he wanted was to get away from her.

"Mnot hungry," he said, taking a big step to get around her. He could see she was a face full of questions and she wanted to talk.

"What's that you got there?" She spoke to his back. He wouldn't turn around.

It was easier when Truman wasn't on night shift because then Shakira had no use for Thulani. She and Truman would sit at the kitchen table and dream their dreams. Shakira was having some sort of difficulties with her pregnancy and was trapped in the house.

Thulani closed and locked his door by wedging the backrest of his chair underneath the knob. He fell into his bed with the cloth still tightly in his grasp. He lay on his back fingering the cloth, thinking that it had been tied around her body. The fine cotton cloth.

He had touched her. The girl. In fifteen or twenty seconds he had seen what girls hold secret, though she did not invite him. Or them. And he had her skirt. The torn cloth. In his bed.

He took the cloth and unfurled it from the tight roll, then spread it into a full rectangle on his bed. It was beautiful. An indigo sea, streaks of violet, drops of turquoise in bolder drops of gold. He ran his hands along the fabric, searching for the girl who wore it. To picture her in it, he had to see it fully open. He took two nails and a hammer from his bottom drawer and began to nail the cloth to the wall facing his bed.

"Thulani! What's that noise?"

He ignored Shakira.

She jiggled the doorknob but could not get in.

"Thulani! What are ya doing?"

"Leave me alone" is what he said, but it came out in a mumble.

"Thulani, open."

He blasted his stereo. Some Wyclef Jean. Finally she gave up.

Shakira didn't really care, he reasoned. She was doing what she thought her role as woman of the house called for. He wished she'd do it elsewhere and leave him alone. He wanted no words tonight.

He hammered the last nail; then he lay in his bed to admire the skirt. He was so struck with the cloth he couldn't sleep. At the Dumpster he could not fully appreciate the colors. The indigo. The turquoise. The violet and gold. But now, in his bed with the lights turned off, he saw the design, which was the pattern of a peacock in full fan. Thulani could not take his eyes off the colors. And in the semi-darkness it seemed as if a hundred golden eyes of the peacock all stared back.

THREE

With the exception of one recurring event, every Wednesday was like every Monday, was like every Tuesday. That Wednesday Thulani rose, showered, stepped into a pair of baggy Bermuda shorts, then went out onto his roof to be with his birds. Instead of sharing last night's dreams with them, he asked aloud, "What should I do about her? It's Wednesday."

For the past five weeks since that night, he had spotted her, the raped girl, coming down Eastern Parkway every Wednesday at eleven-twenty, by the bank clock. The first time he saw her, he felt a strong urge to get to the street, just as he had done that night. Unfortunately, like that night, he couldn't move. He simply let her pass and watched her until she slipped into what had to be

Nostrand Avenue. Then he'd stay on his roof and listen to music, stare at cloud formations, or design bigger dovecotes in his head, until the bank clock showed one-fifteen and she returned from wherever she went.

He knew she would be passing through.

He looked to his birds for advice, resolved to take any hint as a sign and act upon it. Yoli and Dija cooed sympathetically, but this told him nothing. Tai-Chi demonstrated the graceful art of diving for last night's pizza crust but was cut off by Bruno, who swooped down and snatched it.

"What, you crazy?" he asked Bruno. "I'd scare her."

The fact remained, Bruno had the pizza crust.

Thulani turned to Esme, who, as usual, was off to herself. "Hey, Es-may, hey, Esemaay. Hey, girl."

Esme hopped away.

"Don't be like that. Tell me what to do, what to say, you being a woman."

Esme did not want to be bothered. She perched on the antenna.

Thulani waved her off. His birds could not help him, and he had detained them long enough. He watched them fly away under Bruno's lead, banking right, left, and out of sight.

It was early yet. He had time before she would appear. He went inside to take breakfast. His brother,

Truman, had come in from his shift and was off to bed. This left him with Shakira, who was stirring a pot of thick, lumpy, whole-grain porridge. She ate these concoctions whether she liked them or not for the sake of her unborn child. Natural foods were better for the baby, according to Shakira. He grabbed a bowl, his box of Cap'n Crunch, or "processed sugar," and sat at the table.

"Correct me if I'm mistaken," Shakira began, "but I did not sleep with you last night."

Thulani grunted at her, rather than say the "Good morning, sistah dear," she wanted. He watched her pour the glop into a bowl and thought, Vile. She read his face well but joined him at the table nonetheless. He would be content to eat in silence, although Shakira would never let him get away without conversation, sitting face-to-face. She swallowed a spoonful of her porridge, took a moment to clear her mouth, then asked, "Ya have plans?"

He never took this to be a serious question. She always asked this, and his answer was always the same: "Naw" or a head shake.

"Ya let this whole summer go by, no work, no studies, no friends."

"So."

"You're not a child, Thulani. Ya should be planning. Doing. Thinking about college."

He poured more milk and cereal into his bowl.

“Ya drink too much cow’s milk.” With Shakira it was always some new thing she got hold of from books and magazines. She had come to their house touting goat’s milk as “the righteous milk.” Then it was soy milk. Now rice milk.

He knew what to do in this situation. “Could you be looved?,” a favorite of his father’s. His music was there in his head when he needed to drown out Shakira. “Don’t let them change you.” He crunched loud, bobbing his head while she talked on. At this point The Wailers were much too mellow. He switched to Shabba.

Shakira had to know he had left her, although this did not discourage her. After nearly three years of Shakira in the house he knew her litany cold: He was too much into himself. He sat on his roof, talked to birds, got blacker by the sunloads, ate Cap’n Crunch, had no ambitions, no girlfriend, yah, yah. She could talk and talk. None of these things was on his mind. He thought only of her, the girl, and that she would be passing by in yet another hour.

Thulani washed and dried his bowl, watched some TV, then went back up to his roof. It was ten minutes past eleven. He knelt at the edge of the roof, in his “waiting for her” position. He still had not figured out what he would do or say, but he knew he would do something. Perhaps come down off the roof, tap her on the shoulder, and say, "Girl, I've been thinking about you. Are you all right?"

He played this back to himself to get a feel for her reaction. As he tried to picture her expression and what she might say, he realized he had only a distorted face to go by. True, he had filled in his dream girl's face with her face, but he had wiped away her blood and healed her scars.

This made him wonder if she had healed in five weeks. Could he look at her without pausing on her scars? Would she recognize him and thank him for rescuing her, or would she fall apart?

He began to think that trying to talk to her was a bad idea. He was about to step away from the edge of the rooftop but then saw her coming down Eastern Parkway, her head and chest high, her gait proud and undaunted as she passed the alley. She carried a backpack and wore a long skirt that swayed as she walked. He imagined it was much like the skirt pinned to his wall, made of fine silky cotton, except for its single color, bright marigold. As he watched her walking swiftly with her head high, it puzzled him that she was not in hiding and that her colors were so bold.

He followed her for the three blocks with his eyes, not realizing that he had crept along to the other end of the rooftop. It was when she disappeared down Nostrand

Avenue that he told himself he might never get another chance to talk to her. He ran inside the apartment, past a startled Shakira, and was on Eastern Parkway running after her. He stopped to catch his breath at Nostrand Avenue and to see if he could spot her. There were only a few bystanders at the bus stop; not one of them was the girl.

She could have turned on Lincoln Place or gone into a store on St. Johns, but which one? Thulani looked into shops along the block. Although he didn't know her, he couldn't imagine her going for pizza before noon. He didn't glance inside Ayoka's Hair Braiding, for braids didn't require a weekly visit. Besides, she wore her hair pulled up on her head, never braided. He did glance inside the real estate office, the money transfer place, and the music store. No girl in a yellow-gold skirt. He tried the flower shop, this time going inside.

"Yeah, boss?"

"Just looking," Thulani said. "For someone."

The florist's eyes said, Do you see anyone here? Thulani backed out of the store, accidentally kicking a potted plant.

Why was he running after her? This was crazy. He was crazy. Obviously she was all right. She had filed her police report and gotten tested. She didn't need him to ask how she was, remind her of that night, or stare at her scars. She had passed by with her head held high, not offering the alley a side glance. She didn't hide in dark colors. She didn't need him to rescue her.

He decided to turn back, and there she appeared in her skirt, bright and yellow. She had stepped out of a shop on the opposite side of the street and tucked something, perhaps a small bag, into her backpack and continued down Nostrand.

He crossed the street to get a better look at the shop she had come out of. It was a store with Chinese characters painted on the door, and a sign propped in the window that read CHINESE HERBS AND MEDICINE, ACUPUNCTURE ON PREMISES.

He didn't want to go inside; he just wanted to know what it was all about. Thulani pressed his face against the window but saw no one. On the counter sat a mortar and pestle and a set of measuring scales, much smaller than those used in grocery stores. Behind the counter were cabinets with about fifty little drawers, each one marked with Chinese characters.

When the shopkeeper, a middle-aged Chinese woman in a white lab coat, appeared from the back room, Thulani stepped away.

What did she want with Chinese herbs? Why did it take five or ten minutes to prepare? Where did she go next, and why did it take an hour before she returned to Eastern Parkway?

He could see her up ahead. There was a block and a half between them. He took one step, another, and a broad Mother-May-I in her direction. Her skirt movement hypnotized him. The dance of her lean and sensual body made him forget she was a rape victim; she was a girl whose skirt swayed with the sea. Not only did she pull *him* with her motion, but other men turned to watch her walk by.

Thulani wondered if she wore no bra and if her nipples showed against the fabric of her top. Picturing her body in detail made him erect, something that happened seemingly all the time. Girls had aroused him before, but this was different. She was flesh. Warm. Angry. And he did not have to imagine her. He had seen her. Touched her.

Then she stopped abruptly, and he froze, expecting her to turn around. Just as abruptly as she stopped, she continued, only now at a slightly faster pace.

What now? he thought. Run after her? Then what? He only wanted to know she was all right. This was what he told himself as he walked faster to keep up with her.

She vaulted up the steps to some building in the next block. As he approached, he saw it was St. Augustine's, a Catholic church. A statue of St. Augustine, a black missionary in a long robe, held out welcoming arms. Thulani wiped his hands on his Bermudas, wiped his sweaty forehead and face on his shirt, and went up the steps to the Catholic church. He entered the church, but he did not want her to see him just yet, so he stepped into a little room off to the side. The entrance to the room was draped in a maroon velvet curtain. There was a dark screen before him that separated his little room from yet another. Before him were the words "Bless me, Father, for I have sinned" in English, Spanish, and French.

If he remained quiet, he would not be discovered. He would wait and peer out of the velvet curtain until the service was over. When she came out, he would talk to her.

Excluding his brother's wedding, it had been years since he had attended a church service. His mother was Episcopalian. He too was Episcopalian, back when he attended Holy Trinity on Fulton. That was three Easters ago. His mother was no longer with him, and he hadn't been Episcopalian ever since. His brother had become a Rasta, the creed of his father. Now Truman was married and a transit worker. Those were his religions. Work and Shakira. He seemed less and less a brother.

The aroma of incense that drifted from the altar found his hiding place. Through the slightly pulled-back drapes he watched a black priest say mass to the girl and mostly elderly men and women. The priest spoke and made hand gestures, raising his fingers to his forehead, lips, and heart. The parishioners responded in kind. Thulani tried to follow what was being said but could not, for the priest and the parishioners spoke in what he thought was French.

"Haitian," he said aloud. "She's Haitian."

He watched her make the sign of the cross, kneel and rise several times. When they sang hymns, he picked out her voice, which rose above those of the old people, the organist, and the priest. It was a voice that wore bright colors. She then took communion, her pride replaced with humility. When the mass was over, and the priest had left, she went to the altar of candles, took dollar bills from her backpack, and put them in a box. He watched as she lit the tallest candle and knelt, her head bowed, her back curved, legs ending in sandaled feet, making a number two in profile. She rose, dipped her fingers into a ceramic fount, and made the sign of the cross, touching her forehead, above her abdomen, then both sides of her chest. She repeated an anointing of her abdomen and pelvis—something no one else did. She then took a small vessel of some kind, dipped it into the fount, capped it, and placed it in her backpack. Each action she carried out with her head lowered.

Thulani had to get out of there. He slipped out of the confessional and left the church. She would be outside within seconds. While waiting for her in the parking lot, he had made up his mind. No more following her. When she came down the church steps, he would walk up to her and offer to walk her home.

She was awfully fast, or he wasn't as brave as he thought. She sped right past him and was halfway down the block by the time he saw her.

Thulani walked fast. His legs were longer than hers, and his stride was greater. He lost sight of her in front of him and was practically on top of her when she turned around.

"You!" she screamed. Even then her accent was thick.

He was stunned, tongue-tied. Before he could explain or apologize or ask if she was all right, she took off, the backpack bouncing against her. She never looked back.

Thulani vowed to leave her alone and to let her die in his mind. He would no longer care if she was all right, and he would stop filling in his dream girl's face with her face. Her prayers, candles, and Chinese herbs were silly next to his vow.

Before he fell asleep that night, he faced the skirt nailed to his wall and said, "To hell with her."

FOUR

A hot one is what the DJ on the radio promised. Hotter than Hades, damp like mop water. Thulani felt it in the early morning as he watched his birds fly off. He felt the thickness surround him when he looked down on what would be, in an hour, sheer madness. Police stationed barricades along Eastern Parkway. Vendors set up their tents and tables while revelers slowly filled the streets. Madness.

Carnival in Brooklyn—or, as the newspapers called it, the West Indian Day Parade—was nothing like carnival in Jamaica. Back in Jamaica, carnival went on for days and nights. Calypso, socca, and reggae called dancers out into the streets. People gathered for parties in every home. It was a happy time. Even Daddy stopped working long enough to throw Thulani up on his shoulders to watch the festivities.

Up on Daddy's shoulders was a place reserved for Thulani alone. He played with Daddy's long dreads and stuck out his tongue at Truman down below. Riding high on Daddy's shoulders made him tall, tall like the men on stilts.

Sometimes he thought it had all been a dream. Being too little to climb trees with Truman, being chased by a neighbor's goat, or looking up at green hills, as high and far as his eyes could see. Even Daddy, tall and soft-spoken, always smelling of black licorice, seemed a dream man.

If he had been older than three when he, Mommy, and Truman left Jamaica, he would still have his father's ways and voice cut firmly into his memory. He envied Truman for having known Daddy and for showing off the things Daddy taught him, such as how to start up a car, change a fuse, or pound a nail square on with his hammer.

In spite of the photographs of Daddy stationed throughout their home, and all of Mommy's recollections, Daddy remained clouded in smoke and green hills. He had been told that Daddy was "a fine carpenter" and that he built the best cabinets, tables, and coffins in St. Catherine. He had been told that Daddy was the youngest of eight sons and, like Thulani, was his mother's favorite. He knew a great many things about his father, though none of these things brought him closer to his memory. It was only at carnival time that the image of Daddy, the feel of his hair, the licorice chew stick in his mouth, the *clomp-ca-lomp* of his work boots, and his singing as he worked, became clear.

When they first came to Brooklyn, Auntie Desna, who was not a relation but a woman from Mommy's village, took them into her home on Bedford Avenue. In those early days Thulani stayed posted at the door, watching for those work boots to *ca-lomp* through the door. Either Mommy led him away from the door and said, "Daddy will follow," or Truman would hit him for behaving like a baby.

That summer Auntie Desna told them about the West Indian Day Parade. She promised them a good time, saying the parade "will bring you back home." When Thulani saw and heard the familiar things, the men on stilts, the steel drums, the reggae, the dancers in mas, he was sure Daddy would come to him, as he always had, out of the green hills. Year after year Thulani searched the crowd to see if Daddy was out there, caught in the pushing and dancing. Many a time he tore himself from his mother or from Truman to go running after some dreadlocked man, only to be disappointed. The last time he ran after a stranger, Mommy grabbed him and shook him and said firmly—for she never meant to repeat herself—"I begged Daddy to come, but he wouldn't leave. Once Daddy stuck in his safe place, he'll not budge."

Daddy had sent money from time to time and occasionally a card for birthdays. He had even sent Thulani toy animals that he carved from scraps of wood. But Thulani could not remember the last time he had actually spoken to his father. And that was what he wanted. To hear his father's voice.

Thulani looked down on the madness, determined to stay above it. The two times that he felt compelled to come down were both because of her, and he would never be so compelled again. Not after she had run from him when all he wanted was to . . .

He wasn't sure.

He tried to let the girl go. Stop thinking about her. But everything about her opened questions in his mind. What could he do? Nothing. Not even if she went through life thinking he was someone she had to run from.

He couldn't blame her. He had followed her that Wednesday. He had paced his distance so he could enjoy the sway of her hips as she walked down the street. He had hidden himself in the church so he could watch her pray. When he worked up the courage to tap her and speak, she had caught him.

He thought of writing her a letter to explain. Apologize. He thought if she read his words, she could hear his voice and know that he meant her no harm. It would be a deep letter. He would compose his thoughts. Find something that would reach her. Put her at ease, if that was possible. Then he would write neatly. Stick the letter in her mailbox and walk away.

This sounded good until he realized that he did not know her name or where to begin. In his head he said,

> Girl,
> Dear Girl,
> Dear Girl Who Was Raped,
> I'm the one who helped you that night.
> I'm the one who you hit.
> I'm the one who followed you.

No. Not a letter. He had to talk to her. Let her look into his eyes. See that he didn't mean to frighten her. More important, he had to see himself in her eyes and know she didn't think the worst of him.

"Bird bwai!"

It was Shakira. In his room, at his window, trespassing on his peace.

"Thulani, don't make me come up there."

He sighed, feeling the weight of her on him. If she later complained of aches from the stair climbing, he wouldn't hear the end of it from Truman. Before he could get up to answer her, she was standing in the doorway that led to the roof, her arms folded over her belly.

"What?"

"Take down my table."

"Down where? In that?" He meant the carnival mob. "Not me."

"I've been working all summer on my tings," she whined, a sure sign that she would tell Truman. "I have a friend holding my spot. They can't hold it forever, you know."

He was comfortable where he was. He didn't want to face her, let alone answer.

"Ya hear me, Thulani?"

"It's too crazy," he said.

All summer long Shakira had sewn pillows and dolls like those from Jamaica, Trinidad, Barbados, and the Dominican Republic to sell for ten dollars apiece. She called it extra income, but Thulani knew it was busywork while she was housebound. Even Truman did not like the idea of her fighting among the crowd, but she seemed determined to be in the midst of the parade.

Thulani would have been quicker about helping her if it weren't for her attitude. It was the way that she proclaimed herself woman of his mother's house that made him slow to move. It was her expectation that he should come when she called or answer every question she put to him. She was his brother's wife, but nothing to him.

"I'll tell Truman."

Still no reply. As far as he was concerned, she could stand there all she wanted. Threaten. Whine. Stomp. Go into labor, for all he cared. He wasn't going.

"Fine," she yelled up. "Mtakit mdamnself!"

He threw a pebble that hit the TV antenna. That was all he needed—for Shakira to tell Truman how she struggled down flights of stairs with her table, then fought through the crowds.

If Truman had married Shakira to take care of things when Mommy left, it was not necessary. Mommy had taught Thulani everything. He could steam doctorfish, make oxtail stew and dumplings. He could wash clothes to perfection and take needle and thread to any mending job.

Shakira, on the other hand, was hardly a cook, although Truman ate with gusto everything she burned. She was a "neatener," not a scrubber like Mommy. If Thulani wanted the bathroom and kitchen sparkling clean, he had to do that himself.

In spite of the fact that Shakira seemed good for only reading and crowing, Mommy said she was perfect for Truman. When it was clear that they would marry, Mommy gave Truman her emerald ring from Daddy to offer as an engagement ring. To Shakira she turned over hand-sewn baby clothes, recipes, and stories that she had shared only with Thulani.

After almost three years Thulani had no choice but to accept that Truman loved Shakira. He had long given up complaining that Shakira overstepped her boundaries or that her cooking and housekeeping were so-so. Truman took her side in every matter. It was just easier for Thulani to stay on the roof with his birds.

He found Shakira loading her wagon with dolls when he came inside. She smiled but didn't bother to look at him. As he folded the legs of the card table, she could not let the opportunity pass and said, "You know what's good."

The parade was everything he had seen from the roof, except instead of being above the madness, he was surrounded by it. Sheer madness. He and Shakira were lucky to have a spot along the parkway to pitch the card table. There were twice as many vendors as last year.

Stands with codfish cakes, coconut drinks, dolls, flags, and bootleg tapes lined the parade route. The streets were packed with parade-goers—dancing, milling, pushing, and buying.

Though he didn't want to be with her in all the chaos, he could not help but marvel at his sister-in-law. Determined to sell every doll and pillow, she was hardly meek about flagging down potential buyers. While she sold, Thulani fetched mountain springwater—"not distilled, not mineral"—and plates with samples from every other stand. When Shakira was low on change, Thulani went from table to table to break twenties. When she went to the portable toilets, he watched her table. As long as there was no lull, he didn't mind being there.

It became unbearable when after three hours only two dolls remained and passersby sped past Shakira's table. With no buyers to cajole, Shakira turned her talk to Thulani.

"That's a pretty cloth you have."

He pretended not to hear.

"On your wall," she said, begging a reaction, some telltale gesture that she could pounce on.

Heat rose up in him. She had no right to be among his things. To stick and prod him.

"Where did you get it?"

"Nowhere."

"A cloth like that had to come from somewhere."

She had no right.

With one sweep he knocked the dolls off the table.

"What! You crazy? Where you going? You have to help me."

He turned his back to her and was absorbed into the moving crowd. He could hear her calling after him. He wouldn't leave her there to struggle with the table and cart. He'd be back. He just had to step away from her at that moment. He wasn't ready to talk about the girl. Or her skirt. Or the alley. He certainly didn't want to hear Shakira's spin on it. Not while the girl was in his every thought.

He needed his stride to be wide and free, but no one step was his own. He was pushed into a group of female dancers in mas, their buttocks and breasts jutting out of scanty, sequined costumes. Their flesh surrounded him. One dancer shoved him. Someone kicked him. Another dancer teased him, shimmying her breasts at him and sticking out her tongue. He broke free of them and imagined himself running through the hills of his homeland until exhaustion washed away his rage and suffocation. Then he saw a trace of green cloth. Bright, bold, like the green parrots of the Amazon. He saw it as its wearer dashed across the parade route and was swallowed in the thick of the crowd ahead.

His mind raced. Was that the girl in one of those skirts? This was his chance. He had to find her. He began to push through the crowd.

"Eh! You crazy?"

"Hey, bwai. Watch it."

He didn't care. He couldn't let her get away. He knew what he wanted. Her name. He had to know her name. She took up almost every thought in his head. He needed her name to go with his thoughts. And to talk to her. And maybe smell her. To be close to her for a minute. Everything in him stood up large. His heart, his voice, his longing. He could not let her go.

Although he lost sight of her green skirt up ahead, he had to believe she was there. He would have to swim through the throng, ten-man deep, just to reach her. His heart was beating in his ear. What would he say when he caught her?

He tried to see the back of her head, but it was impossible. The crowd was too dense. The people, all dancing, pushing, milling. He couldn't get through. He jumped up high, but the Jamaican float was passing through, its carnival priestess imploring the masses to jump up, jump up. He could not find the girl or her green skirt.

In his head he heard his mother say, "Still yourself.

Just be still." He had to trust this voice. Even if he got to the girl, he couldn't just rush her. He would scare her. He would have to do it right. Approach her carefully. Let her see him coming, if that was possible. Let her decide if she wanted to talk to him. If she ran from him again, then and only then, would he let her go.

He made his way through a cluster of blue and yellow T-shirts. If he could only get around the next group, he would be in front of her. He couldn't see her too well, but he caught glimpses of the bright green skirt.

He somehow had to get ahead of her.

He saw his chance and ducked under a blue wooden police barricade and ran ahead. A police officer blew his whistle at him, but it was okay. He was now in front of her. He slipped back under the barricade before the police officer came and stood at a stand of figures carved from coconut skins. She would not miss him.

The Jamaican float pushed on, and its priestess took the crowd with it. Steel drums clanged in his heart as he waited.

She was coming, surrounded by friends. They had stopped to get a better glimpse of the oncoming Trinidadian float, and he feared she would cross to the other side of the street. But she didn't. She was headed for the table.

"Hey," he'd say, and nod as she passed by. If she didn't give him a rude look, he would know everything was all right and one day, if not today, he could approach her.

She was coming. He had to be in her direct path, so he stepped out before her. As the people who surrounded the girl in the bold green skirt unpeeled themselves from her one by one, she caught his eye and smiled at him. But it wasn't her.

FIVE

The sun peeled open his eyes as he lay in his bed. He had overslept. He had no place to go but up to the roof and free his birds.

An hour earlier he would have slipped downstairs and eaten his cereal unnoticed. As it was, he could hear Shakira telling about the comedies and splendor of carnival to Truman in an excited patois. Thulani himself no longer spoke patois, thanks to a prekindergarten teacher, a strict Jamaican woman, who advised his mother to speak only proper English, if he was to succeed in school. This start-and-stop talking of trying to speak proper English confused him. He would raise his hand in class and speak only to have his tongue cut off each and every time. It was easier to be quiet.

To enter the kitchen, Thulani stepped over Truman's legs, which were extended outward, a deliberate obstacle. Stepping over Truman was a "little brother" toll he paid, since Truman clearly would not move. Offering them both a morning greeting was yet another toll. They reminded him at every opportunity, We are your elders, not your equals.

He got his cereal and milk and sat at the table. Between Shakira's expanding belly and Truman's long legs, the room was too tight. Knowing Truman was watching, he poured his cereal, then scooped a handful into his pants pocket.

"There you go, feeding those birds with my food."

"Don't fuss with Thulani," Shakira defended, in a mock tone for sure. She was still fanning herself with the money she made at carnival. "I couldn't have sold my dolls without him."

He wouldn't give her the benefit of a smile. If he hadn't returned to help her pack up her table, she would be telling Truman how he had thrown a fit at her and knocked down her dolls.

She placed two ten-dollar bills in front of Thulani's bowl, waited for him to acknowledge her gift, then counted and re-counted over three hundred dollars with her stubby fingers.

Thulani felt their eyes preying on him, like a cat

waiting for a sparrow to make the wrong move. He wouldn't touch the money.

Shakira chattered on about the parade while she made out a deposit slip to their cherished savings account, the window of their dreams. Truman insisted that she treat herself to a dress or perfume with the money, but Shakira wouldn't hear of it. Every cent was going to their nest egg. Their dream house in New Jersey.

They weren't speaking to each other but to him: This is what responsible people do, Thulani. Save for the future. He ate his cereal.

Shakira drummed her nails on the table to get Thulani's attention. "Go collect the rent from Dunleavy. Take the rent and our carnival earnings straight to the bank."

With a mouth full of cornflakes he said, "Ask me."

"She just did." Truman was firm. End of discussion.

Thulani shook his head.

"And you might want to take a dollar or two from your earnings and deposit it to your savings account." She was trying to sound like Mommy.

He refused to look as if he were considering her suggestion. It did not matter. Truman held on to Thulani's savings book, and it would snow in hell before his brother let him see it, let alone draw from it. Having him ask for every dollar was how Truman kept him underfoot.

"You can't just spend, spend your money," Shakira said. "You must put something away."

This was precisely why he was slow to pick up the money. If the twenty dollars was his money, then it was his alone to do as he pleased. If it was theirs, they should keep it.

Truman pointed to the bank envelope. "That's a lot of responsibility we're giving you," he told his brother. "A lot of trust."

Thulani put the bank envelope in his pocket but left the two tens on the table. It was not the first time he had deposited Dunleavy's rent check. They were making a big deal for no reason.

"There's a party at my sister's," Shakira said. "Come with us."

He looked up at her with his mother's almond-shaped eyes.

"My cousins will be there, and it will be nice. Plenty of food. Music. Dancing."

Shakira and Truman exchanged looks. They had been discussing him. Again. He did not have to actually hear these talks to know what was said. "Sixteen and no future, no plans, no friends." "Get him a job, a woman, and kill those birds. That will set him straight."

At Truman's urging, which consisted of a look, lips pursed in a kiss, and a slight turn of the head, Shakira left the room.

"Hey. You."

Thulani looked up.

"Shakira's been tellin' her cousins about you. Talkin' you up good."

He meant her female cousins. The ones his age. Thulani shrugged.

"You're sixteen, braa. Dead is dead."

Thulani cut a look into his brother.

"I no stuttah," Truman said. "Let go of Mommy. Live your life."

"She was our mother. I can't erase her."

"No one said erase," Truman said. "Just grow up. Be a man. Mopin' won't bring back Mommy. Mommy gone, Thulani. Mommy dead."

What did Truman know or feel? By the time Mommy left, Truman was twenty and had climbed out of his youth into manhood. He had met his wife-to-be and had passed the test for the Transit. He had only to deal with the grief of losing Mommy and not the pain of needing her.

From the time Mommy announced that she was flying home to Jamaica for a short while, Thulani had begged to go with her each and every day. He seemed to exhaust her, but she remained firm about leaving him behind. She had to visit Daddy alone. Thulani would come home another time. She said good-bye at the airport—nothing too emotional, just a kiss and a hug—and she was off to their home in St. Catherine, where the hills were covered with trees, and the rains poured down, the sun broke through the mountain peaks, and Daddy waited. There she spent three weeks with Daddy, while he cared for her and built her coffin.

Mommy always said she had three lives: her past life in Jamaica, life with her sons in Brooklyn, and the life to come. Thulani never sought to understand the riddles she spoke in. When he was thirteen, and his mother began to speak in riddles, he cared about video games, briefly for a girl who flirted with him in class, and about his music. Only Truman and Mommy knew that she was dying. Only they knew that this was a kiss good-bye.

There was no telephone in Daddy's house, so Thulani wrote letters to let his mother know he was no longer angry she had left him behind. How many letters she actually read he did not know. Truman let him mail those letters, make a Mother's Day gift, and talk of "when Mommy comes back" until one day Truman just said it: "Mommy died two weeks past."

Thulani had watched her get on the plane and

watched the plane take off. It had not occurred to him that she would not return.

"Mommy had cancer, and she went home to die. That's it," Truman continued.

"You should have told me."

"And what could you do? What could I do? She was gone. Before our eyes."

Anger had Thulani by the throat. He didn't speak for a time. Then he said, "You knew good-bye was good-bye."

Truman stood up. He didn't have much use for this kind of talk. He said, "The party's at Shakira's sister. We're all going early to help out."

Shakira materialized to say, "And take a hot, hot bath. I don't want anyone smelling pigeon shit."

Only when Truman and Shakira both went to their bedroom did he take the twenty dollars. He went up to the roof and unlatched the crates. His birds had been locked in for too long.

He asked for their forgiveness and sprinkled the gold flakes he had in his pocket onto the tarp. "I'm gonna build you a dovecote like no other," he promised while they clamored for the cereal.

He watched them fly off into the final days of true summer. In a week he would be one of a thousand lost heads locked in school, roaming the halls. Already he mourned the warm kiss of the sun on his face, arms, and chest.

He knew he would not go to the party with Truman and Shakira. The lure of good food, music, and Shakira's pretty cousins could not disguise what the gathering was about. An attempt to grow him up. Have him think family, earning, contributing, marrying one of those she-cousins one day soon, and taking root in a house in New Jersey with his brother and Shakira.

Thulani knocked on Mr. Dunleavy's door and waited. Dunleavy moved slowly, relying upon his walking stick, which Thulani could hear tapping against the floor.

Thulani dreaded collecting the rent. Mr. Dunleavy would never simply hand him the check and let him go. The old man always wanted to show Thulani an old camera or photographs of Jamaica. Mr. Dunleavy had made his living as a photographer, taking pictures for newspapers, magazines, and even postcards. The photographs covered his walls.

If Mr. Dunleavy did not try to interest Thulani in photography or Jamaica, he always spoke of Thulani's mother. That he had known her when she was a schoolgirl, no older than Thulani.

Mr. Dunleavy cracked the door ajar. Thulani thought, The snow came down hard on a man, an expression his mother used. Dunleavy's hair and mustache were completely white.

To Thulani's relief, Mr. Dunleavy had the rent check in his hand.

"Not feeling too well," Mr. Dunleavy said, giving him the check. "You run along."

Instead of going directly to the bank, he went to the big library at the edge of the park. He pulled two books from the shelves—one on carpentry and another on bird habitats. As he sank down in the stacks and flipped through pages of dovecote designs, he lost track of the bank, the party, the plane, and his mother.

He studied the architecture of these mostly open-faced cubbyholes and thought of ways to add a protective screen with a latch. He needed a door of some kind to lock his birds in at night. How else would he free them in the morning?

He returned the books to their shelves and left the library. It was after two-thirty. He had to cut through Prospect Park to make the deposit at Carver Federal. He couldn't dally at the fishpond, or linger over the orchids—orchids his mother said grew like weeds in her garden in St. Catherine.

He hurried along, thinking of the deposit envelope in his pocket. Then he stopped. Before him, cutting across the park, he saw a sway of color, a bouquet in the breeze. It was a skirt—lavender, yellow, green, and blue. This time he was not deceived by his eagerness. *It was her.*

SIX

Don't run, don't run, don't run, is what his heart said, each *thump-thump* a plea to both himself and to her. If he rushed her in all of his excitement, she would run. If she ran from him, he'd have to let her go, even if he never got to know her.

He tried to slow his pace, but she was too near. Sooner or later she would feel him behind her. He called out, "Hey!" louder than he intended, but she didn't turn around. He tried again. "Hey, girl in the—" He stopped, tongue-tied on those colors she wore. A rainbow of them. Still nothing. She had to know he meant her. There was no one else in the park but them.

He watched her. Her skirt billowed. Her hair was gathered on top of her head, which she held high. Just as he remembered from those Wednesdays from the roof. If she saw him and smiled, if she saw him and smiled . . .

He ran out of small steps. When he was abreast of her, but not too close, he said, "Please don't run."

She gave a side glance and said, "You." She was suddenly real, not the blur of a face he'd color in minus scars, but a face full of disdain and beauty that up close he could see he had gotten wrong.

"Look. I didn't mean to scare you that day."

Her eyebrows, thick and arched, said, Me, scared?

For nearly two months he had been rehearsing this moment. He had been sitting on his rooftop practicing his speech for Yoli and Dija; Esme didn't care. He had been lying on his bed in the dark, apologizing to the skirt nailed to his wall. Suddenly no words could be enough to offer this very real, angry girl whose quick, mad glances speared him. All he could do was walk with her and hope to find himself and say what he needed to say.

She cut another look at him and tossed her head. He loved her hair. It was thick and rippled like hair that had been braided and unbraided. In spite of that evil glance his first thought was to touch it.

"I don't like how you follow me," she said. "Everywhere I turn, there you are. What do you do—watch and watch me?"

He wanted to say no, but he didn't lie easily. He did watch her at every opportunity.

"*Stop* following me."

"I—I was going this way when I saw you coming across the park."

"Oh? And you was going to St. Augustine's? To get down on your knees? Say 'Hail Mary, don't put fruit in my womb?' Yeh?"

He was struck dumb by her and couldn't come quick enough. Everything about her threw him off. Her lips, her eyebrows, her hair, her blunt little nose.

When he couldn't answer, she gave him yet another look of disgust and walked away.

He stayed with her, which only annoyed her, but he had to speak now or forget it. "That day . . . at your church . . ."

She stopped.

"I'm sorry."

He waited for her to speak, to accept his apology but she said nothing. Since she didn't walk away from him, he kept talking. "I don't want you to think the wrong thing about me. Ever since that night . . ." Her eyes stopped him cold. It was too late to take it back. "I—I'm just sorry. . . ."

"Why?" she snapped. "Did you do it?"

He shook his head no.

"Then keep your sorry."

Nothing was as it should have been. She was supposed to recognize him as her savior. They were supposed to be joined by that bad night like survivors of an airplane crash. In his dreams they embraced. She cried in his arms. He said everything was all right.

"I wonder about you," he said softly. "All the time."

"What you need to know?" Her fury spun out at him. She, the girl who knelt so humbly with her head lowered, was in his face. "You know everything of mines. You see everything of mines. What else you need to know?"

"That you're all right."

"I'm fine. See?" She twirled on her heel, flipped her hand at him, then walked faster.

"Hold up," he said. "I'll walk you through the park."

She gave him eyebrows. *Why?*

"Make sure you're all right."

"Ha. What you gonna do, protect me? Look at you." She had the nerve to smirk at his lanky, unmanly body. "You can't do nothing."

She was hitting him again. Stinging him. And like the night he charged down from his rooftop, he let her.

"I'd at least try."

Again her face said, *Why?*

There was nothing left to lose. In another fifteen

minutes he would miss the bank's closing time. She was already disgusted with him. Nothing mattered.

"I can't stop thinking about you," he told her. "I wonder if you sleep at night or if you toss and turn."

She didn't react.

"I wonder if you went alone to be tested. If you was scared when you told the police."

She laughed, "Ha!" Big. Loud. From that laugh he knew she had done neither, and now he was disgusted with her.

"I don't understand you, girl."

"Ha, ha. What a big surprise."

"You go for Chinese herbs and to church, but you can't report it?"

"Why go to the police?" she said coolly, almost singing. "Did they come when I cry out? What can they do? Get back my stuff?"

He wanted to be mad at her, but she was right. Even he would run from the police before he'd run to them. But she should have done something, he thought.

"People should know," he said. "We could put up flyers."

"Flyers. Ha."

She was trying to make herself seem older, laughing at his innocence. It only made him angry.

"That's good," he said. "Laugh. Take herbs. Get on your knees. Pray."

"Leave me alone." She walked faster, but he easily matched her stride. He had not found her after all this time so he could fight with her.

"Look. I'm sorry, girl, I'm sorry," he said until she slowed her pace. Even so, she wouldn't look at him.

"I spoke out wrong," he said. "You've been through a lot. I want you to know, I'll go with you to get test—"

"They don't have nothing on me!" she said, swatting him away with her hand. "They don't have their dirt on me, their babies on me! Nothing."

"I'm not saying—"

She turned and stuck her finger in his chest. "I take care of my business. I cleanse my blood. I don't need no one telling me about test."

You can't be clean. I saw you.

He regretted thinking it, even for that second, for it was as if she could see the reflected image in his eyes of herself lying naked. She struck out at him with her fist, wild and off-balance, but he anticipated it and caught her balled hand before it made impact. She regained her footing and pushed him with both hands.

"You think I'm filth? I am disease? Then go! Get. Leave me. I don't need you. Leave me. Just leave me alone!" And she said more in Creole.

"I don't think that. I only meant . . ." And he gave up trying to explain what he himself didn't understand.

"Just leave me alone."

"I can't."

She pushed him.

There was never any peace around her. Instead he felt sick and brave at the same time, ready to jump into the unknown only to be hit.

"I'm walking you home."

"That's what I don't like. You don't ask. You just follow me."

"Can I ask you now?"

"Ask me what? I don't even know you. You're a stranger. A strange boy."

"Can I walk you through the park?"

"If I say no?"

"Then that's that. I'll stand right here while you go."

"And you won't follow me?"

He shook his head no.

"And you will stay out of my business?"

He nodded.

"Say it."

"I'll stay out of your business."

"And you will leave me alone?"

"You'll never see me again."

"You promise? Your word?"

"My word."

There. He lied to her. His most solemn word he gave her, and he lied. It wasn't as hard a thing to do as he thought. He would always hope to find her and hope she would want to be found.

"My name is Thulani."

She said "Tulani," low enough so he could hear she did not pronounce the *h*. And they finished their walk in silence.

Once beyond the park and back in the world with everyone else, they watched out for cars and dodged people. The bankbook still in his pocket jabbed him. He knew he'd have to face Truman and Shakira when he put the undeposited money on the table. Their ranting would be endless, but it didn't matter. He was going to walk her, the girl, as long as she let him.

When they got to her house on Franklin Avenue, she said, "Now go," but he waited at the curb while she put the key in the door. As she opened the door and the window curtains parted, then closed from inside, she turned to him and said, "I am Ysa."

SEVEN

Every morning after he set his birds free, Thulani walked to the corner of Franklin and waited across the street from her house, hoping to catch Ysa on her way to school. His heart would say, Go to the buzzer, call out her name. After all, he told himself, they were hardly strangers. They had talked. They had argued. She had given him her name—something she wouldn't have done unless she intended him to use it. Even so, he couldn't bring himself to her door to press the buzzer. For a month he stood in the same spot from seven o'clock until eight watching the window curtains part occasionally. Then he'd leave for school.

He didn't give up once inside school grounds. He took to roaming the halls of Erasmus Hall High, peering into classrooms from door windows on the chance that he would see her. He'd press his face against the glass and look for her hair, a mass of ringlets piled on her head, or even better, he'd seek out a rainbow among the rows of browns, blacks, and grays. Color would lead him to Ysa.

He roamed the halls during first and second periods and wondered how he could have missed her before. She could have been there all along, walking down Eastern Parkway as he stood above her on his roof. She could have been one of those who gave him "cut eyes" when he bumped into her in the hallways. He had been in a fog and hadn't seen what was in front of him. Since the time his mother died, no one existed. No one—except his birds—could touch him or be with him. Then there was Ysa. The girl whose scream pulled him from sleep, whose naked body wore his jersey. The girl who both rendered him speechless and drew him out. Out from his roof, out of his silence, out where he heard his own voice. Out of himself. All he wanted was to find her, touch her, talk to her, be in the world with her.

"Where your pass, son?"

Thulani released the doorknob and faced the hall patrol. He *could* run, but he had been caught. It didn't matter. "Don't have one."

He was promptly thrown into detention.

The next day he did it again. Peered into the windows of classes in session, hoping to find her. He observed hundreds of girls sitting in classrooms. Pretty girls wearing jeans and tops the colors of fall. Girls in curls and braids, short hair, ponytails, hair up, hair down. Girls writing in loose-leafs, passing notes, or staring at chalkboards. Some had even smiled at him, catching him off guard and making him feel good. But as pretty as they were, none of these girls was her.

He had only her name, Ysa, to go on and where she lived. He had no last name, although he was quite sure she was Haitian. He knew that she surrounded herself with color, believed in herbs, confession, and prayer and that her little breasts would fit his mouth.

He also knew he couldn't continue like this, hanging outside her house or roaming the halls hoping to find her. He decided to seek out some Haitian girls and describe Ysa. As big as it was, the school had a decent representation of Haitian students. Surely someone knew her or attended mass with her at St. Augustine's. Haitian students stuck with one another the way Chinese stuck with Chinese, and Pakistanis stuck with Pakistanis. If he had to go up to every Haitian girl to find her class schedule, he would.

In his social studies class he spotted Janine Desravines,

a girl he remembered from elementary school and junior high. Janine had always been a fairly popular girl, always the center of her group. If anyone knew Ysa, she would.

He tried to get her attention at the end of social studies, but Janine and her friends were already out of the classroom. He followed them out to their lockers and called her by name, but she didn't respond. He knew she was messing with him, but he didn't care. He wasn't going away. Finally one of Janine's friends, a girl in brown, tapped her and pointed in his direction.

"There's this girl," he said quickly, because all eyes were on him. "Haitian girl. Lives with her mother or grandmother on Franklin. Wears a lot of colors."

Janine and the three other girls giggled. It was the kind of thing girls did well. Cut a man down to size. If he had to take their abuse to find his girl, he would. "Her name is Ysa. Do you know her? If she goes to Erasmus?"

Janine conferred with her group in Creole, tossing her name, Ysa, up and down in what he felt were derisive tones.

"You sure she's not Jamaican?" Janine asked.

They all giggled.

"She's Haitian."

Janine shot back something, and she and her friends burst out laughing.

He started to walk away.

Janine called after him, "No. We don't know your Ysa."

Later in the cafeteria Janine sat next to him while he drank milk and said, "You know Julie?"

"Julie?"

She gestured to the girl in the brown top.

"She thinks you're okay."

He blushed, then smiled, not expecting this at all. That someone would think he was cute.

"While you're looking for this Ysa, you should think about it."

Janine rejoined her group. They began talking excitedly and giving him face, particularly the girl in brown, Julie. They wouldn't leave him alone until he smiled back.

He did not go first to the roof as he usually did when he got home. Instead he flew upstairs to the bathroom, locked the door, and stood before the mirror to see what he had. To see why Julie smiled at him and told her girlfriends she thought he was okay and why Janine was bold enough to tell him so.

In the mirror he saw his mother's slanted eyes. Her long lashes. Her lips as he remembered them, well defined and full. Not so much from memory, but from the photo in his bedroom, he saw his father's prominent features, his strong nose and jawline, red brown complexion smoothed over high cheekbones.

He smiled at his endowments. He had looks a girl could find attractive.

Since the age of thirteen up until nearly sixteen, his face had been eclipsed by hooded sweatshirts. Even through hot summers he wore hoods. He would have worn them the past summer if not for a police sketch of a mugger that appeared on the news. The robber, a black male between the ages of sixteen and twenty, was armed and considered dangerous. He vaguely fitted Thulani's height and build and committed his crimes wearing hooded sweatshirts. Before the broadcast was over, Shakira had broken through his door, gathered up every hooded sweatshirt he owned, and stuffed them into a Hefty bag, which she set out with the trash. "They round you up first, ask questions later."

If he wasn't so angry at Shakira, he might even have laughed.

There was a knock on the bathroom door. "Thulani. I have to get in there."

"I'll be out."

"You've been in there an hour. Let me in."

She exaggerated. He'd been in there five, ten minutes.

When he finally opened the door, she pushed him out and closed the door to pee. With her belly even larger she was always in the bathroom.

He went downstairs to wait for her. Today he decided to give her what she always wanted: in. He was going to talk to her. Ask for her opinion.

Shakira had changed clothes and appeared to be a little flushed, but Thulani let these things slip his notice.

"Suppose you like a girl," he began, though Shakira seemed preoccupied, putting away her still warm but unserved dinner. "But she's kinda hard, uh, hard to know. Then there's this new girl."

Even preoccupied, Shakira wouldn't spoil this opportunity. He'd never give her another chance.

"First Girl givin' ya hard time?"

He nodded.

"Ya sure New Girl like you?"

"Yeh."

"Ya like New Girl?"

"She cute."

"Which one on your mind?"

"First Girl."

"Then stop triflin' with New Girl and call Truman."

"Truman?"

"What, I stuttah? Call him. Tell him to get to the hospital quick. Then call the EMS."

"Hospital?"

"I tried to wait, but I can't go no longer."

Thulani did not do things in the order that Shakira had asked. First he ran up to the roof to leave the cage open for his birds. Then he called 911 for the EMS. They asked him questions about the contractions, blood, and water—questions he couldn't answer. They said they would be there in fifteen minutes. Then he called the dispatcher's office at the subway station to leave the message for Truman.

The EMS ambulance came in thirty minutes. They took Shakira's pulse and put a stethoscope on her belly. Thulani wanted no part of it when the female driver raised up her skirt. He waited outside until Shakira came out on a stretcher. The EMS driver said the baby was not crowning but they should get to the hospital quick.

Thulani locked up the house and rode in the ambulance with his sister-in-law. Every five minutes she dug her nails into his arm. He was relieved when they arrived at the hospital and Shakira was wheeled away, glad when Truman finally arrived.

Two hours later he was an uncle and Truman was a father. When Truman emerged from the delivery room, his stone face broke and tears gushed. Thulani had never seen his brother cry, not even during the time that

Mommy went away. Died. Truman said the baby girl was healthy, she looked like Shakira, and they would name her Eula after Mommy. He gave praises to Jah, then told Thulani, "There is but one child in our house. You have to help out. Get a job."

EIGHT

For three days Thulani knew the peace of a quiet home. Everything was as his mother intended, with both sons caring for her home. Thulani cooked and did laundry while Truman painted Eula's room. Once the baby was brought home, Shakira's family would visit often, so the house had to be ready.

During this time Truman never repeated what he had said in the hospital or asked his brother how the job hunt was going. This was not Truman's way. He stated himself plainly and once. Even though he ate Thulani's oxtails, wore the shirts that Thulani washed and ironed, and likened all of Thulani's housework to their mother's, it was understood that Thulani was to seek work.

On the morning that Shakira and Eula were to come

home, Truman said, "I've been thinking." This meant that he and Shakira had been discussing this new thought in detail and it was now time to bring it to light.

Thulani waited for the other shoe to drop, and at that moment he fully comprehended the expression. In Truman's pause he tried to match the tone of Truman's last word with the many possibilities that could follow. He thought of the many things Truman and Shakira could devise and held his breath.

"You show no inclination for school," Truman began.

He could breathe freely. This was true. He spent more time roaming the hallways looking for Ysa than sitting in class taking notes and fretting over the SATs.

"Mommy left you some money for college."

"Yeh, so?"

"The money will be better spent toward a down payment on a house in Jersey."

"What? Leave Brooklyn?"

"A child canna grow on concrete. We need a house with a yard."

"They have homes with yards in Brooklyn," Thulani said.

"We're leaving Brooklyn," Truman told him.

"The brownstone's worth money. Mommy always said—"

"It needs too much work, Thulani. Who's going to

do it? I'm selling the brownstone. In two years we're gone. End of discussion."

Is this what Truman and Shakira did at night? Thought of ways to choke him with their plans? Steal Mommy from his memory? Kill off his birds?

Truman put his plate in the sink for Thulani to wash. He said, "You'll be eighteen before long. Old enough to be responsible with the money Mommy left. That money plus my share will make the down payment until we sell the brownstone."

The other shoe landed. There was nothing left to say.

Thulani ran up to his roof to unlatch the dovecote. Even though he had no morning treats, no cereal or seeds, his birds still gathered at his feet and perched on his arms and shoulders. Bruno landed on his head. He needed to surround himself with their cooing, their feathers.

Leave Mommy's house? Leave his birds? Leave Brooklyn? And leave Ysa—if he ever found her again. He couldn't leave yet.

He took Yoli to his heart and stroked her breast feathers. When she grew restless in his grip, and Bruno became jealous, Thulani let her go. He let them all go.

Shakira and Eula were home by the time he came in from school. He wanted to get a good look at his niece, although it was impossible. Shakira did not let her child out of her arms. Even when her own mother, sisters, aunts, and cousins warned her Eula would be spoiled, Shakira never turned her eyes from her daughter.

With much reluctance Shakira brought Eula to the nursery and placed her in her bassinet. While Shakira was being catered to by her family, Thulani saw his opportunity. He had seen the baby but wanted to have this moment alone with her.

"Look at you," he whispered. "Just look at you." Truman was right. She was the very picture of Shakira but with Truman's eyes. Before Thulani could reach down into the bassinet to hold her, the door flew open.

"Cha! Ya crazy or what? She's had no shots and you smellin' like pigeon shit. Gwan from her!"

For five days Thulani cleaned, cooked, and did homework while Shakira rested and fussed with her baby. Once Shakira was ready to resume housework, Thulani went back to his rooftop or went looking for Ysa at the Chinese herb store, St. Augustine's, or the park. When he thought of it, he approached storeowners in his neighborhood for after-school jobs. Although these inquiries for work were halfhearted on his part, he knew he could not continue to live off his brother's earnings. With the addition of Eula to the family, his life changed. He was suddenly a man, expected to give up everything he knew simply because he had no plans of his own.

In class he drifted in and out of the finer points of bacteria and trinomials. He flirted with Julie but dreamed of Ysa. Nothing held his interest longer than fifteen minutes. School was simply the sitting place. Sitting and longing. Longing to be elsewhere, and having nowhere in mind.

He would do enough work to be promoted, then graduate the following year. If he couldn't keep himself in school, he would take the GED exam. He might have tried college for a year to please his mother, but she was gone, and he couldn't envision a lecture hall as a place to be, only a place to sit.

For now he needed a part-time job. Any job would do. Just something to put money on the table once a week for his share of the groceries. If he didn't find a part-time job on his own, Truman and Shakira would find work for him.

He took the bus downtown to scout out possible employers. Most fast food-places welcomed him, but he did not crave hamburgers, and he would be knee-deep in burgers. He thought about the big library at Grand Army Plaza, but this would keep him indoors. He needed to be outside. Perhaps get work as a messenger.

That would take him around town without a boss to breathe down on him. He found a place on Flatbush, but it already employed too many foot messengers. Did he own a bike? No? No job.

After two hours of filling out applications and hearing "Check back in another month," he gave up. No one wanted to hire part-time help, even if he would soon be seventeen. They wanted either a diploma, a GED, or some experience. Or the jobs just did not appeal to him.

Maybe he should leave school. Take his GED by the summer. Get full-time work, but not with the Transit. Truman worked long, crazy hours and didn't laugh anymore. No hospital work either. Nothing near sickness and death.

The stores were closing. He took the Flatbush bus and got off a few stops before his house. He had been out all day without so much as a drink of water. But he didn't want water. He wanted something sweet, quenching, and filling. He imagined the taste of Ysa's lips. If he could kiss her lips, he would want nothing else.

"Eat all the strawberries, all the mangoes, but don't touch the so-so-plump berries."

This is what his mother said when he fished around the fruit bowl not knowing what he wanted. His mother made up fruit that grew only in her homeland on

Nanny's trees. The so-so-plump berry was such a fruit. It could be eaten only once in a lifetime, for its sweetness was hard to tolerate. "Make sure you truly want it," Mommy warned. "Once you suck the fruit, nothing will ever taste sweet again."

He walked on, looking in stores, thinking, Wet and sweet, wet and sweet. Then he came upon Yong Moon's Fresh Fruit Market and headed that way in spite of what Truman had said.

Nearly three years ago Truman had told him never to buy from Yong Moon, following an incident at the fruit stand. Mr. Moon struck an old man he caught stealing plums. No matter how hard Mr. Moon had struck the old man, the old man held on to the plums, and the dark plum blood oozed between the old man's fingers. The gathering crowd turned on Mr. Moon, pelting him with grapes, peaches, and limes from the outdoor carts. Mr. Moon's wife, a tiny woman, then ran into the crowd swinging a baseball bat in every direction. For two weeks after the incident the community picketed Yong Moon and his wife, but the fruit eventually won out. Yong Moon sold the best produce in the neighborhood, if not all of Brooklyn. No one could picket Mr. Moon forever.

Thulani saw Mr. Moon, himself an old man, struggle to push the melon cart into the store. Halfway up the ramp Mr. Moon stopped to massage his shoulder. This was an opportunity. Thulani crossed the street and pushed the melon cart up the ramp and inside the store. It was all too easy for him. He pushed the citrus cart inside as well.

"I need work," he told Mr. Moon.

Yong Moon said there was no work.

Thulani just stood there while Yong Moon stacked empty crates. He followed the man. "I can push these carts in, no problem."

Mr. Moon said nothing.

"I can stand right here and watch the store when it gets busy."

Mr. Moon was deaf.

"I can wash down the sidewalk," Thulani said.

Yong Moon went on stacking the wooden baskets as if he were alone.

Thulani looked to the back of the store where the register was. Mrs. Moon was not there. She hadn't been there for a year.

"I can come after school. Three to six."

Yong Moon said, "Close at seven."

NINE

Thulani wanted to tell someone other than his birds about his job, but there would be no one when he got home. It simply wasn't enough to hold his conquest inside. He was overwhelmed with a need to be with someone and talk.

Eventually he would tell Truman and Shakira about his job but not just yet. They had a way of sucking the joy out of a thing with their insights and too many questions. Instead he would walk in one payday and put all his money on the kitchen table, pour his cereal, feed his birds, and not be reminded of where the cornflakes came from.

He didn't have to think hard about the money he'd earn or if taxes would be extracted. He expected a minimum wage and to be paid under the table. It was hardly the kind of money that would make him independent. However, the part-time work would provide him with a few dollars he wouldn't have to ask for.

His stomach growled from emptiness. He had left the fruit stand without buying so much as a banana. The last thing he wanted was to eat at home, out in the open, where Shakira could question him about his progress on his job search. He'd rather grab a bite out in the street, then go up to his room and close his door. He stepped out to the curb and looked down the block to see what was still open. It was either the pizza shop or the Chinese takeout place. He felt in his pocket for a ten-dollar bill, his lunch money for the next three days.

As he walked toward the pizza shop, he saw a girl wearing a gold-yellow jacket the color of a bodega awning, coming in his direction. She carried a wide, flat black case, the type used to hold posters or artwork. It was the way she walked, the head just so, the hips a nice sway, and that bright yellow jacket. He was already smiling.

"Ysa."

She sort of acknowledged him.

"Hey, so . . ." Where were his words? He couldn't find them. Her eyes almost glared at him. "Where you coming from?"

She shot daggers at him. "None of your business."

He gave her a wounded look, one so pathetic she almost smiled. This look had in the past been effective on his mother when she initially said no.

"All right," she relented. "If you must know, I'm coming from Paterson Silks. I cut fabric."

The excitement of just getting a job and having her there made him say, "I'm coming from work too. At Yong Moon's." He pointed in the direction of the store.

"Oh?" she said, doubtful. "You? For Yong Moon? You're not family." She was right to doubt him. Even the lowliest positions at family-owned businesses stayed within the family.

"I work there," he insisted.

"Hmp. I don't ever see you there."

He smiled sheepishly, both pleased to know she was a regular customer at Yong Moon's and embarrassed to have been caught in a half-truth.

"I just started."

He was thinking, If I could keep her here talking, when his stomach growled. She turned up her nose to show that she was disgusted, but he would not be deflated. He tilted his head to the pizza shop, raised his eyebrows, and asked, "Slice?"

"No, no," she said. "I have supper waiting."

He gave her those eyes again, with more of a plea, for he remembered that he was cute, a workingman, and was feeling quite invincible standing before a girl he had once rescued.

She said okay.

Thulani paid for their pizza and fruit punch with his lunch money and carried their tray to the table where she sat, her huge black case leaning against her side. He watched her pat down the greasy pizza slice with one napkin, bite the tip only, chew, and wipe her mouth with another napkin. He was content to have her with him eating pizza she didn't want. One day he would take her hands, kiss her lips, and put his tongue in her mouth. As he watched her do everything just so, entranced by her slender fingers, her manicured nails, he knew she would be his first everything. For now, seeing her this close and noting her habits was good enough.

"I've been looking for you, Ysa."

Her eyes flashed at him upon hearing her name.

"I wasn't worried," she said confidently, but not smiling. "I knew you would find me."

"I've been by your church, hoping to find you there lighting candles. All I saw were little old ladies praying. Then I went by the Chinese herb place and asked about you. I said, "'Have you seen this girl . . . wears every color in the rainbow?'"

"No, you didn't."

He nodded yes. "I even tried to find you in school. Been thrown into detention every day since September looking for you."

"I don't go to your school."

"You know my school?" he asked.

"No, no, boy. I don't know your school. I go to a *special* high school. And you—pardon me—don't look special."

He showed her he was wounded.

She laughed at him. "Don't give me that face," she said. "Besides, you know where I live if you want to find me."

He shook his head. "I'm not knocking on your door. Not with your grandmother—" He wasn't sure. He just knew the woman behind the curtain, the one who cursed him, looked too old to be her mother.

"Tant Rosie?" She explained that Tant Rosie was her grandmother's sister. A grandaunt.

"Whoever she is," he said, "she wanted to kill me."

"She was scared for me. That's all."

"Scared for you? She was beating you."

"Beat? Ha! No, no. You exaggerate."

He exaggerated about being a workingman. About being thrown into detention every day since September. But he remembered the woman's slap. And Ysa's sobs from the other side of the door.

"All I knew was I couldn't do nothing. I was worried. Scared. Wanted to protect you, girl."

She looked about as if anxious that they could be overheard. Suddenly her confidence was gone. He could see her scars.

She said, "We can talk about something else."

"I'm sor—"

"Forget it."

Then they said nothing at all. Thulani took a big bite of his pizza before realizing she would never finish hers. Once he was through eating, she'd want to leave. He was desperate to make conversation. Anything to keep her there, sitting with him for a few more minutes. He wondered if she would care that he had just become an uncle. Or that he had called the EMS and ridden with Shakira to the hospital. Then he thought, talk about having babies might upset her, a girl who took herbs and teas to cleanse her body when she thought that she might be pregnant or worse. He could tell her about job hunting. How every store manager said no and how Yong Moon finally gave in. But he'd have to admit that he had not actually worked today, and she'd never completely trust him if she knew he had lied.

He could tell her she had pretty hands, but she might run away, like the girl who used to come to him when he daydreamed on his roof. If he dreamed the wrong thing, the dream girl was gone. Maybe he'd say the wrong thing to Ysa.

"Tulani." She broke the silence. "That's too pretty for you. A girl name."

"My mother"—he hadn't said "Mommy" or "my mother" to anyone except Truman—"named me for her favorite poet."

He could see Ysa found that amusing, which he didn't mind, mainly because she still wanted to talk.

"Go ahead," Ysa said. "Say some rhymes."

He laughed. "Not me."

"I know," she said with a certain satisfaction. "You have no art."

"But you do." He returned her smugness.

She didn't catch on. She said, "I'm studying to be an artist. Not like you think, painting pictures. I'm going to design clothing. Do fun things with textiles."

"Textiles?"

"Cloth," she said. "Cloth to move in. Dance in. Be free."

Her face lit up when she talked about cloth. This enthused her in a way he could not understand. Instead of truly listening to her words, he followed her lips. She wore lip gloss. Not pink, not orange, but that color in between.

He had to snap himself out of it, or she would think he was strange.

"Is that what you have in that black case?"

She nodded and said it was her classwork from Art and Design High School, where she was in her junior year.

"Let me see."

"No," she snapped.

"Why not?"

He reached to playfully take the portfolio, but she pulled the case toward her. Her eyes were serious. Thulani let go of the case and said, "I'm sorry."

She let the moment pass and said, "You can see if I say so."

He put his hands up.

"You can't just grab," she scolded.

"I didn't mean anything."

"And your hands are greasy. That is my work. My work. I don't want it ruined."

He started to apologize for the second time. Sometimes he was talking to Ysa and then *she* would appear and stand between them. Rape Girl. Show her scars. Take something the wrong way. No matter what, he felt he had to apologize, whether he had done anything or not. He had felt this before. The night he ran and ran and ran. The time he followed her to her church.

She wiped her mouth and hands. She was done.

He said, "I knew you were an artist or something."

"Why?"

"Only bright, bright colors for you, Ysa," he said, watching her take a self-conscious check of herself, as if it had not occurred to her. "Every time you step out, a rainbow must die."

She sucked her teeth and said, "Crazy boy."

"That's how I find you."

"What?"

"First everything around me is drab. Dead. Then I see bright this, bold that, and poof! there you are."

"So. I like color." She stood and picked up her case. When she turned the black case on the other side, he noticed the letters *YB*, done in silver Magic Marker, in fancy loops. Her handiwork for sure.

They strolled toward Franklin, her street. There was still warmth in the mid-October air. It was a beautiful night. Even more beautiful than those summer nights when he lay on his rooftop, dreaming of a faceless girl. A beautiful night was walking slowly with someone whose hand he could not yet take. And having the air smell so good.

Thulani was careful of how he pointed to the black case; he didn't extend his arm fully. He was afraid she would run away if he touched her by accident. "*YB*?" he asked. "What's the *B*?"

"Baptiste," she said. "My, uh, name."

"So that makes you Haitian."

"How do you know what I am?" she snapped.

"That accent," he told Ysa and Rape Girl.

"You don't know my island," she sang. Rape Girl had stepped aside. It was just Ysa.

He said, "I can guess."

"Hmp." She tossed her head and took a few steps ahead of him. "My island's small, but not poor."

He caught up. "Do you *parlez Français*?"

"Creole," she corrected with pride. "Not like you think. A *different* Creole."

"French Guyana?"

"Ha. French Guyana's not an island."

They were at her brownstone. It was time to say good-night, but he didn't want the night to end, and he had run out of French-speaking countries.

"Before you go," he said, "can I see you again?"

"I'm too busy," she said. "School. Work. Study."

He was not discouraged. The playfulness in her voice was still there. He asked, "Can I walk you to school?"

"I take the train."

Not a no, he told himself. "I'll ride with you."

"You crazy? You'll be late for your school."

The curtains opened. Tant Rosie stood behind the windows, but this time she did not close the curtains.

He shrugged. *So.*

"I leave too early for you."

"Like six-thirty?" he asked.

"Yes. Like six-thirty. And Tulani," she said sternly, "I don't like to wait. I wait, I'm gone."

"I'll see you in the morning," he said.

She told him again that he was crazy.

He waited for her to go inside, then listened for a slap or a scolding from the other side of the door. He heard nothing. Then he went home.

TEN

Thulani set the alarm for six o'clock and stared at the peacocks' eyes on his wall until they blurred into fireballs floating on a sea of plum wine.

When the alarm went off, he showered, brushed his teeth, greased his hair, and examined his face to see what she would see. He had laid out his clothes the night before. He dressed, grabbed a spiral notebook, took two subway tokens from his nightstand, then ran out of the house.

He was a block from Franklin when he stopped walking. *His birds.* He had not given a thought to freeing them, scattering cereal to feed them, or telling them his dreams. He had to unlatch the dovecote.

Thulani turned and started back toward Eastern

Parkway, but he stopped before he reached the end of the block. It was six-twenty. Forget the birds for now, he told himself. If he was late to Ysa's house, she would leave. Think him inconsiderate. Not give him another chance.

He ran down to Franklin and started to cross the street. Out of the corner of his eye he saw a figure in a bright-colored jacket, carrying a large black case and hurrying in the opposite direction. He called after her.

"Y-SAAA!"

She didn't turn around. He ran to catch up with her.

"Ysa." He was out of breath, his heart pounding from making that dash, then pounding more from suddenly being with her.

"Oh, it's you," she said. "I looked for you and didn't see you. I said, Good. I don't need no one to slow me down."

"I'm here," he said.

"That's your business if you're here or not. I didn't ask you to come."

"Don't be like that. I said I would come."

"What you want, applause? I'm late for school."

She pissed him off. He hadn't jumped out of bed while the sun still napped to take this abuse. He was tempted to walk away, but got over this quickly and followed her to the train station.

"Look, if you don't want to see me"—what am I doing? he thought, but couldn't stop himself—"I'll leave you alone." He could lose her, right here, right now.

She swiped her student pass and went through the turnstile.

"I don't want to be looking out of the window to see if you're coming. I don't want to say, Where is he? Like I said, if I have to wait, I'm gone."

He dropped a subway token into the slot and pushed through the turnstile."You said, '*like* six-thirty.' It's not even six-thirty yet." He surprised himself. He heard his own voice, strong like Truman's when he argued with Shakira. He didn't know where it came from, but it was there inside him.

The bell rang for the outbound D train. She said, "My train," and ran down to the platform. Pride held him where he stood, but only for a moment. He had already paid for the ride. He went after her.

The train was pulling into the station. He was amazed to find the platform crowded with students and working people so early in the morning. She was easy to spot, in her colors. She was already standing at the edge of the platform before the car door. He pushed through the swarm gathered at the middle car where she stood and tapped her on the shoulder. The car door opened.

Ysa grabbed his hand and pulled him in, shoving him to the corner of a two-seater. She took the outside seat, stood her case against the side, and unstrapped her backpack.

He didn't know what to say.

"I need this seat," she said, "so my portfolio will fit here on the side."

The doors closed, and the train pulled off. He couldn't tell if he was still pissed with her or if he was feeling good, sitting next to her. It all melted into one warm stream that ran from his heart to his ass. A sweet burn. What his body knew as simply being with Ysa.

"Where are your books?" she asked.

He took out a spiral notebook from the waistband of his pants.

"And?" she demanded.

He shrugged.

"That's it? You don't read? You don't study?" She rolled her eyes to show her disgust or to show off her lashes.

He shrugged and tried to make himself comfortable in the corner seat, but there was nowhere for his knees to fit. He would have to lean one knee against hers.

She took out a book from her backpack and said, "If you don't mind . . . ," and began to read.

It was just as well. He hadn't thought of anything to say. He only wanted to see her. Be with her. Take in her smell, which consisted of coconut oil from her hair, flowers and citrus at her neck and ears, and powder from inside her jacket. Although he was happy to have her knees and arms brush up against him as the train rumbled and shook, he didn't want Ysa to disappear into her book, thinking him a late-coming, going-nowhere lagga head. He wanted her to know he had responsibilities.

"I forgot to do something," he told her. "That's why I'm late."

She looked up from her textbook.

"I have birds that I let out every morning," he told her. "See, I was so exci—well, I forgot to let them out. I went back, but then I knew I'd miss you—"

"You have birds, in a cage?"

"Not in a cage," he said, defending himself. "In a home I built them when my mother—when I was thirteen."

"And you have to let them out? Every morning?"

He nodded.

"So they're locked up. Caged?"

He shook his head. She didn't understand. "Every evening they return to their home, on the roof."

"The roof?"

She looked at him with anger. He was sorry he mentioned the roof. Sorry that he looked too deeply into her eyes, eyes that refused to blink. Sorry he did not know the right thing to say. Still, he tried again.

"They're pigeons. Mostly white," he said. "They're beautiful. Well, the hens are beautiful." Tai-Chi might not mind being called beautiful, but Bruno wouldn't stand for it.

"Hens?"

"Female birds," he said. "The males are bigger, have thick necks. They're called cocks." It was too late to take that back, *cock*. He kept talking. "I started with three white hens—Yoli, Dija, and Esme. I found them on my roof and took care of them when they were tiny. Left by their mother."

"How do you know she left them?" This was almost an attack. A man reading his Dow Jones gave her a sharp look.

"She never came back," Thulani answered. "I waited."

"Maybe it's because you touch them and the mother smell you on her babies," she said, still on the attack. "You're not supposed to touch them."

He felt steam. He only wanted to let her see that he cared for something, even if they were birds. Like everything else he tried, this backfired. She was appalled or disgusted. There was nothing he could say to change what she thought.

The train creaked to a complete stop and sat outside the next station. The conductor blamed the delay on a sick passenger up ahead and promised that the trains would be moving shortly. Ysa turned back to her textbook, Thulani to the posters. Three minutes passed. The other riders accepted this delay, but Thulani became restless, heaving sigh on top of sigh. Should have set them free, he thought. Three, now four minutes were too long a time for someone who did not ride the trains. Too long to be trapped. Too long to feel that the person next to him would rather be with her book because she could only make a sound of disgust when he spoke. He heaved another sigh and stamped his foot.

Ysa tapped his hand and said, "What is that bird that makes that 'oooh, oooh'?"

"You mean an owl?"

"I say 'oooh,' not 'whoo.' *Oooh.* You know. Brown, big eyes. Oooh, oooh."

"Mourning doves," he told her. "I don't have any mourning birds. Only rock doves. Pigeons."

"I had them," she said.

"You?"

"Not how you think—in a cage," she said. "There was

this pair outside my window. Male and female. They come to my window ledge every morning. First he comes with straw and twigs and puts them down for her. Then she sits on the nest, and he covers her with his body and his wing. He turns his head to my window to say, 'Ey, what you looking . . . this is our home. You, don't look at us.' Then he turns to her to say, 'I will shelter you, keep you safe.' I hear them every morning making their promises outside my window. Oooh, oooh."

There was no dark tunnel. No train delay or people hanging over them. There were only her lips, which he followed. Oooh, oooh.

He thought of how protective Bruno was with Yoli and said, "I will shelter you . . . he mean it, you know."

"Ha! That is what you think," she said, breaking the moment. "I see how narrow the ledge is. That it can't support the nest."

"No?"

"Of course not. The wind keeps blowing it away, but this doesn't stop him—what do you call him, cock? Every morning he comes with his leaves and twigs, then shows her the new nest and puts her there. 'Sit. I will shelter you.'"

"What happened?"

"What you think?" She showed some disgust, which

he now realized was sometimes her natural expression. "She got tired of him building that foolish nest and telling her to stay there." She opened her book again, and the train lurched forward. "He still comes and sits at my window. Every morning by himself, oooh, oooh."

ELEVEN

Thulani rode the train back to Brooklyn and pictured Ysa's lips opening and closing. *Oooh, oooh.* Even as evil as she could be, he was ready to kiss her. If she fell into his arms, closed her eyes, and gave him all that she held tightly to herself, then she would be his. He'd never have to wonder when he would see her next.

By the time he reached his block, second period had already slipped away from him. He imagined Ysa's look of disgust if she learned he was late, and for a passing moment he wished he cared the way she did about her studies. He would at least arrive in time for fourth period. This was better than missing school altogether.

From the other side of the street he could see a blue-and-white ambulette parked before his house. All of his longings for Ysa were knocked out of him in that instant. He trotted toward the house. It could be Eula choking. Or Shakira or Truman. He reached the walkway just as Mr. Dunleavy teetered slowly down the steps. He held on to a lady's arm with one hand and his walking stick with the other. Thulani stood at the curb and waited. When the old man came upon him, Thulani saw Mr. Dunleavy's age in the morning light. How frail he was. That each step took a great deal of effort.

"Mr. Dunleavy," he said, taking the hand that held the cane.

Old Dunleavy did not speak. He just nodded and looked at Thulani with twinkling eyes, as if this were all he could muster. He was then helped into the ambulette by the lady, and they drove off.

Thulani ran past Shakira, who nursed Eula in the kitchen, and went up to his roof to unlatch the dovecote. He expected Bruno and the others to flock to the opening and charge at him all at once, but they didn't. It was still early, about the time he'd free them during the summer when he slept late. Even though he had left without freeing them, he did not try to make amends or tell them of last night's dreams, which by now were fuzzy. Nor did he tell them about his train ride with Ysa. Instead he kept these things to himself while Yoli, Dija, and even Esme cooed and clucked about him.

"What happened to Dunleavy?" he asked Shakira. "Fell ill?"

Shakira gave Thulani an incredulous look. "Ill—yeah. It's called age, Thulani. Old age." She unplugged Eula and switched her to the other breast. Thulani no longer turned away. He was used to finding Shakira with her housedresses open and Eula attached to her.

"The social worker took him to a nursing home. He's not coming back."

Thulani was not close to Dunleavy, but he knew he would feel his absence. At the same time it didn't seem fair that Mommy was young and gone, and Mr. Dunleavy was still creaking along, as old as he was. Ten years ago Mommy said Mr. Dunleavy was no younger than eighty, no older than eighty-five. Not even Mr. Dunleavy knew his exact age. He had been born in the hills of Jamaica and never had his birth recorded. It was by the events he recounted in his chats with Mommy that she deduced his approximate age. Thulani used to squat on the floor with his head leaning against his mother's calf, while she and Old Dunleavy sipped tea and talked about the lush green hills of home and the people they knew in common. Even when Mommy left and Thulani occasionally collected the rent, Old Dunleavy made it a point to tell him, "You must visit the homeland while it's still so beautiful." From time to time Thulani considered going to St. Catherine to see his father and the home he left. He'd quickly remember his mother was buried near his father's house, and he'd abandon those thoughts.

Shakira looked up at the clock.

"No school?"

"There's school," he answered.

"Well? Why you're not there?"

He almost said, "I was riding the train with Ysa," but he smiled instead.

Shakira took off the diaper draped over her shoulder, exposing her breast, and gave him a good snap on his torso. This sudden motion startled Eula, whose hands flew up, though it did not stop her from nursing.

Shakira shook her head. "Stupid bwai."

He grabbed his notebook and left for school. Shakira had him up in a girl's room, grunting and sweating and making babies. It wasn't her fault, he thought. How could Shakira know that everything about Ysa made him smile and exasperated him? That she gave him reason to get up in the morning and be in the world. That every day was an opportunity to win her, and he had everything to look forward to—talking to her, making her laugh, taking her hand, and reaching that point of knowing they were meant to join. Why wasn't he at school? Because for one forty-minute train ride, he was that much closer to knowing Ysa.

He walked in on a film during health class and found his seat in the back of the room. It was an AIDS film. He laid his head on the desk and watched a video game depiction of an immune system under siege. He drifted off to sleep.

Janine, Julie, and two other girls approached him during the change of classes.

"So." This time Julie spoke first. "Did you find her yet?"

Thulani said yes.

Janine then added, "Did she want to be found?"

He smiled.

"Look, he's blushing."

Every other day he looked up and saw her at Yong Moon's, among the plantains, yuca, and avocados. Never the oranges or the grapefruits. She never looked up to find him or wave, so he always made his way over to her. Depending upon what she'd pick out—plantains, mangoes, batatas—he'd guess. . . .

"Haiti?"

She'd say, "Don't be too sure."

"Martinique?"

"No."

"I've got you now: St. Lucia."

"You have nothing. Give up. You don't know my island."

As long as she came to the market to buy a dollar's worth of plantains, yuca, onions, peppers—little things she could get at any corner market—he would not give up. Sooner or later she would come to the market and not buy anything.

He continued to meet her in the mornings. He'd rise, free his birds, and run to her house just to walk her to the train station and take the ride with her. He didn't have much to say. Neither did she, but they rode together, and she seemed pleased to see him, though it was not her way to say so.

That Monday of the second week of riding the train he offered to carry her portfolio, but she said no. While she read her book, he took out his notebook and finished his math homework.

On that Tuesday he fell asleep on the train and rested

his head on her shoulder. She didn't push him away.

In the meantime postcards from the Department of Attendance came to his house every day stating, "Thulani Wright was absent periods one to four," on such and such a date. Truman said nothing about the absences, but Shakira wouldn't let them slide, warning him that any girl who would keep him from school was not worth the time she stole from him.

On Friday Ysa stopped him at the turnstile before he could drop his token into the slot.

"Tulani," she said strongly.

"What?"

"Go to school."

"I'm going."

"Now."

"Why?"

"I need to study in the morning," she said. "You distract me."

They were tying up the turnstile, and commuters wanted Thulani to move.

"So you don't want to see me."

"That's what *you* say. I say I need to study."

"I'll go to school if . . ."

"If?"

"If I can see you."

"You'll see me," she told him.

The bell sounded. Her train was coming.

"Tell me again."

"You'll see me," she said, then ran down the steps to catch her train.

TWELVE

"You waste my water," Yong Moon said.

Thulani had been standing over the red leaf lettuce with the hose, watering one head of lettuce until a leaf separated from the head. He looked up and turned off the hose.

"She's not come today," Mr. Moon told him.

He had to face it. Once again Ysa had disappeared. Just when he had a grasp on her laugh, her ways, her smell, just when he was so close to kissing her—a near possibility he could taste—Ysa vanished.

She wouldn't let him ride the train with her, and she was never at Paterson Silks to walk home in the evening. She stopped coming by the fruit stand altogether.

It had been different when he thought of her and did

not know her. Her absence made him wonder who she was. Now that she was within his reach, her absence gave him pain.

He crushed a grape between his thumb and index finger. He didn't have to go through this. There were other girls at school who flirted with him, although he never took them up on it. He could just as easily like any one of them.

Thulani crushed another grape.

He hadn't done anything to offend her. If anything, they were becoming closer. He felt it happening. Why should he seek out another girl when the one that he wanted was right there?

He had to talk to her that evening. If she was suddenly afraid to leave her house because of the ones who raped her, then he would be there to protect her and do whatever she needed. If he found out that she was all right but didn't want to see him, he'd have to face reality and leave her alone. Either way, he had to know.

He gave Mr. Moon three dollars for a bouquet of field flowers, a bunch of blue flowers that clung to the stems. Mr. Moon shook his head no and pushed the money on the counter toward him. Thulani also shook his head no and slid the money to Mr. Moon. This went on two more rounds until Thulani took his flowers and left the money on the counter.

• • •

Thulani pressed the buzzer and waited. His grip on the bouquet was such that he bent one of the stems. When he left her house, he would have either a girlfriend or no one.

The door cracked open. *"Oui?"* came from the other side of the chain. The door opened fully and revealed Tant Rosie, a short, squat woman wearing a somber housedress, her hair pressed flat and neat against her head. Ysa, he noted, had none of her aunt's traits.

"Can I see Ysa? Is she here?"

Tant Rosie waved her hand from side to side and said, "No, no."

"Is Ysa okay?" he asked.

The woman only repeated, "No, no."

He was about to walk away when he heard an exchange from behind the door and recognized the other voice as Ysa's. The door opened. Ysa's eyes greeted him first, bright and welcoming; then she spoke. The pain he had felt earlier vanished.

"Hello."

"Hey."

She waved him in, then uttered something in reassuring tones to Tant Rosie, who backed away from the door.

"I hope you don't mind that I came to see you. . . ."

His voice trailed off, hoping she would cut him off and say, "Don't be silly." Instead she eyed the bouquet, which he had forgotten. He offered it to her.

"Winter flowers," she said as she took them. "I don't like these so much. They're not so pretty." She examined them with her nose scrunched up. "You don't have to bring me things."

He was too glad to see her to be offended. "My mother told me to bring a gift when you visit someone's home for the first time."

"I never heard that one," she said, and led him inside.

Tant Rosie said something entirely uncomplimentary about *le fle* as she took them from Ysa to put in a vase. This he knew by the lengthening of her otherwise round face. He imagined she said, "You see? He is bringing flowers because he wants your pussy. Don't be a fool."

Tant Rosie beckoned them both to the kitchen. "Come. Sit. Eat," she offered in her limited English.

He took in everything about the house, hoping these things would tell him more about Ysa. Except for a mounted crucifix whose fake rubies and emeralds sparkled on the wall—but not so much the faded portrait of a haloed Christ—he did not sense Ysa's touch in the home. The knickknacks, the blue-and-white ceramic grand duke and duchess lamps, the crocheted afghans spread across the plastic-covered couches told him more about Tant Rosie.

He searched for decorative plates or straw mats, any souvenir to proclaim their island, but there was nothing of that sort. Ysa seemed to know that this was what he was looking for as he turned his head in every direction, and she gave him her telltale grin that said, "You don't know my island." He grinned back: "I'll know soon enough."

When he was sure the old woman could not hear he whispered, "She said you weren't here."

"No, no. You misunderstand." Ysa defended her aunt. "She was telling you it's too late for you to come." Ysa pointed to the clock. It was almost eight.

His mind returned to that first night when he stood outside the door and heard the slap. "She won't hit you . . . me being here?"

Ysa laughed—a laugh he knew well. It was how she lied to him and pretended everything was all right.

Tant Rosie placed a small plate of rice and beans, or, as Ysa said, *riz collés*, with a few slices of plantain before him. He nodded his thanks to her, hoping she would disappear after she served the meal. Instead the woman sat in a corner with a crochet hook, yarn, and a watchful eye.

Thulani ate the food. He was hungrier than he had realized. Within minutes Tant Rosie put another plate before him. He held up his hand—"No, no"—but she would not hear of it. He cleaned this plate as well.

"I hope you don't mind me coming to see you." Again he sought Ysa's absolution, but she only ate. "You don't come by the market."

"I don't need any fruit or vegetables. We have enough."

"You don't let me ride with you in the morning," he said.

"I told you. I need my train ride to study."

Tant Rosie took his plate away and washed it. She was smiling but speaking sternly to Ysa in Creole. Ysa nodded to her aunt.

Thulani had to know once and for all. If she told him what he didn't want to hear, he'd leave her alone.

"Am I bothering you, Ysa?"

"Bothering me?"

"Is it, you don't want to see me?"

"I see you now," she said, but would not look at him.

"I think about you every day."

"Don't say this nonsense." She glanced at her aunt.

Thulani thought, Let her hear what I'm saying. I don't care. He told her, "I think about you riding the train in the morning."

"Ha! You are asleep when I am on the train."

"I think about you wrapped up in one of your rainbows." He referred to her skirts, the ones with many colors.

She kicked him under the table. "Sssh."

"I don't see you—"

"I have exams," she said. "I cut back my hours at work so I can study."

"And that's why I don't see you?"

"I'm trying to get into a top school for design. It's very competitive."

"So you study all day and make . . . designs?" He didn't know what else to call it.

"How can I explain it to you?" She gave him a look, then seemed to come to a decision. "Stay," she commanded, then left him for a moment and returned with her portfolio, the one she would not let him touch.

She unzipped the case slowly, peered at him, still weighing her decision, then opened the flap. "I'm going to show you sketches. Ideas. You understand? *Ideas.*"

He reached to touch a page, but she pulled the book away. "No, no. Your hands are greasy. I'll turn." While he listened, she turned the pages and explained each sketch, all done in lead pencil. She pointed out the differences in sleeves, why these were hard and those were easy. She showed him necklines, cuffs, darts, and pleats, and he sat and listened to every word. She was completely animated until she came to a particular page that she turned quickly.

"Hold on," he said, wanting to grab her arm, but he didn't. "Not so fast."

She let go of the page but covered the sketch with her hands as it lay flat on the table.

Now he had to see it. "Please?" he asked.

Tant Rosie stood up to see what was going on.

Ysa removed her hands.

It was a drawing of a carnival dancer in full mas. The previous sketches had been drawn in gray pencil, but this was done in colored pencils. Reds, golds, turquoise. The dancer sprouted white and gold wings. She wore a jeweled bra and matching mask. Even though the limbs and neck were exaggerated, Thulani could tell the body was Ysa's.

"This is . . . wow."

"You like it?"

He nodded.

"My country never has a float in the parade. If we did, we would not wear costumes like this. We would wear the long skirt, maybe. But carnival should be free! A grand spectacle. I would wear this!" she said of the drawing.

"I'd never let my girl wear that."

Ysa closed the case and pulled the zipper.

"I'm not your girl," she snapped, then put the case aside and turned her back to him.

This was too much work. It was too hard. And as she put it, she wasn't his girl. Thulani rose and pushed his chair in.

"Look, girl. I'm going to leave you alone."

"That's good," she said. "Leave me alone."

He said, "Good-night and thank you" to Tant Rosie, who was at the door, eager to see him off.

"Yes, good-night," Tant Rosie said. "Good-night."

THIRTEEN

He made sure he caught her eye in homeroom and again in third period and in fourth. He meant to approach her after class, but she and her girlfriends made a quick exit to the cafeteria. Probably to secure their lunch table. They sat in the same spot and had to get there early.

He stood on line for a turkey sandwich and milk. They were already sitting and talking when he spotted them. He thought he stared too long until Julie gave him a big smile. He made his move and took his lunch tray to her table.

"Mind?" he asked.

Julie smiled and tilted her head. She had pretty hair. A beauty parlor style. Straight with curls on the end. She was neatly put together. A shade of rose pencil outlined her lips. She had light green shadow around her eyes. Mascara. Manicured nails. A girl.

"Julani? Bulani?" Janine snapped her fingers between each guess.

"You know my name."

Julie came to Janine's aid and whispered his name.

"Oh, *oui. Pardon,*" Janine said. "Tusoso."

"THU—LAN—EE."

"Yes, that's it," Janine said. "It's just . . . I don't hear it so often in class."

"No, no, we always hear that name," another girl, Mona, cut in. "'Thulani, no homework again? Thulani, absent again? Thulani, speak up. Thulani, detention.'"

One by one, Janine, Mona, and Yvette threw questions and petty insults at him while Julie hung back, speaking only with her eyes and an occasional laugh that came out through her nose. He didn't mind their game. In fact he expected to endure her friends' humiliation ritual before he could talk to Julie alone. Janine told him he looked better without those hoods he used to wear. Mona said his dreadlocks were getting too long and he should cut them. Yvette asked if he would ever cut his lashes. They were too long and pretty for a guy.

He came quick enough with his responses but was

careful not to go too far. He was allowed to defend himself, but he could not mortally offend any of her friends in the process. When Janine felt they had done their duty, each girl picked up her tray and left Julie alone with Thulani for the remaining twenty minutes of the lunch period.

As they talked, or he told her what she wanted to hear (how she stood out among her friends; how he was waiting for the right time to approach her), she told him what he wanted to hear. Mainly that she would not make things hard for him. This she did with her eyes.

He fell into a rhythm with her, feeling the ease of talking without the fear of saying the wrong thing. As he sat with this very willing, flirtatious girl, he learned the truth about him and Ysa. With Ysa he dreamed and wanted, pushed and pushed, but Ysa never asked for any of it.

On the other hand, Julie, who took his hand to critique his nails and scribbled her number on a scrap of loose-leaf paper, was his for the asking. To be sure there was no misunderstanding, he later asked her in homeroom, "Will someone mind me talking to you—besides your girls?"

She laughed. "Yves and I broke up." She waited for some reaction, but he gave none. "*Yves.* Soccer team Yves. Do you play soccer?"

He shook his head no. Truman had always been the cricket and soccer star in the family. His mother used to make snacks for Truman and his teammates when they came to the house after soccer matches. That was a long time ago. Sports never appealed to Thulani, particularly if his mother wouldn't be there to cheer him on.

"No? No soccer? What do you play?"

"Nothing."

Then Julie took him by surprise. She pushed up his jersey sleeve and felt the biceps on his right arm.

"So hard. Firm."

He had been seeing Julie for a few weeks. He and Julie walked home together, trailed by her girlfriends. Each time he hoped they would run into Ysa and catch jealousy on her face. She was never anywhere in sight.

He was messing up at work, always late or always asking for days off to spend with Julie. The last time he asked for a day off, Mr. Moon threatened to let him go.

He learned to be prompt where Julie was concerned, and he always treated her friends to soda and french fries. He learned that movies made for a safe date, as he never had to make too much conversation, and he usually let her pick the movie.

He ate dinner at Julie's a few times, sometimes with her family, though they were seldom home. Her parents worked off-hours, and her brother was in college. Julie gave him his first kiss, and after a month, and a Christmas gift (an ankle bracelet that she pointed to in a store window), she took his virginity in her bedroom while Janine, Mona, and Yvette stood guard downstairs. He removed his pants, but she removed only her panties, keeping on her skirt. She put the condom on him and guided him inside her. When it was over, Julie came downstairs and hopped on the sofa with her friends as they began rapidly talking in Creole. Thulani followed, fully clothed. In English Julie said, "Three, four minutes," to Janine's question, and the girls laughed.

"She *is* pretty," Shakira said, holding Eula belly-down across her thigh. She rubbed small circles on the baby's back to burp her. "But she's not the one."

Thulani cut his lashes at her. *How do you know?*

Delighted that she might possibly know something, Shakira explained, "The way you bring her here. Introduce her to me. Have her sitting watching videos out here in the open."

"Yeh, so?"

"If Thulani has a piece of music, he plays it on his Walkman for self and self alone. If Thulani has some special ting, a photograph or clipping, he hides it in his heart away from the gazes."

This was all true, for the one thing he would not share with Shakira or anyone else was the cloth of a hundred eyes that still hung on his wall. Even when she saw it, he refused to explain what it meant or how he got it. Only one person would instantly know what the cloth was, and she would never see it again.

"Julie is something special to me," he insisted, though they both knew he lied. He kept her out of his room because he could not bring himself to take down the skirt.

"Don't get me wrong," Shakira said. "The girl is nice. Just not the one you've been sick for."

He had to laugh, his only way to dismiss her. As far as he was concerned, Shakira knew nothing.

"Remember?" she said. "'Sistah Luv, suppose I'm stuck on one girl, but another girl won't leave me 'lone?' Remember I told you? Leave the silly girl to her silliness, be a man, and step to the real one. Then I went to the hospital and push out Eula."

He laughed hard, throwing his head back. He hadn't laughed, really laughed, in so long.

In the nearly two months that they saw each other, Thulani never mentioned his roof or his birds to Julie. When he had to open the dovecote, he'd say, "Look. I have to do something." He brought her to Yong Moon's only twice after school. If he took her to his house, she'd sit in the living room where all could see her. When she hinted about seeing his room, he had his excuses ready: Shakira would not allow it, or it was a mess.

Once he got the hang of sex, he thought he could screw Julie forever. They had ample opportunity at her house, and she enjoyed it. Even though his body was always ready, the want of her faded. The thinking of her. The list of things he liked about her did not seem so extensive. Her treasures. These all faded. So even as he entered her, joined with her, and rode her until he was finished with her, he did not want her.

Julie was not completely without dignity, nor was she blind to his lack of interest. She was back with Yves shortly before Valentine's Day. From his rooftop Thulani saw them walking arm in arm when he went to close the dovecote. He wished he cared.

FOURTEEN

"Shouldn't his family do this?"

Thulani had just come in from taking another large garbage bag out to the Dumpster. Going out in the rain didn't bother him as much as what they were doing, raking through Dunleavy's things. Before the sun came up, Truman pulled him out of a warm sleep and said, "We have work to do, braa." No further explanation.

Truman threw another stack of magazines onto the pile but offered no reply to his brother. They had been in Dunleavy's apartment since the hard rain started falling early that morning, clearing out cupboards and closets. In that time they accumulated two heaps: one of clothing that would be donated to charity and the other of what Truman called junk.

"This isn't right," Thulani said. "Us being here. Throwing out the man's things."

It was the third such remark he made about being in Dunleavy's apartment and the third time Truman didn't answer. Finally Thulani got the message. Mr. Dunleavy must have died in the nursing home, and there was no one else to dispose of his things. Why Truman couldn't have said in the first place that Dunleavy had died, Thulani didn't understand. It was like Mommy dying. One minute Thulani was talking about her, counting the days until her return; then suddenly he learned she had long been gone. The difference was he felt sorrow about Mr. Dunleavy's death, but no pain, and he was glad of that.

Truman tossed a cardboard box onto the heap that would be bagged as garbage, spilling some photographs on the floor. Fascinated by the photos and bored with the task of bagging garbage, Thulani stopped to pick them up.

There was not one color print among them, just old brown and yellowed prints, not even black-and-white. The surfaces of the photographs were matte, and some of the borders were scalloped. To Truman's displeasure, Thulani sat cross-legged on the floor and thumbed through stacks of photographs in the cardboard box. He'd feel the surfaces of the prints, then turn over each photo to see the dates stamped on the back. The fairly recent pictures, at least twenty years old, had been taken in Brooklyn. He recognized the shops and streets. The older photographs, however, were of Jamaica. Even without the greens and yellows he knew his homeland. The place where his father lived and where he had run free as a little boy. It seemed an unspoiled place.

He came across a photograph of three schoolgirls in their best pinafores, gathered on the steps of the school with their teacher and principal. This was not the kind of picture that would normally interest him, except for the middle schoolgirl in plaits, who had his eyes and Truman's nose. Surely this was his mother or at the very least an aunt. He pointed out the girl to Truman.

Truman gave the photograph a passing glance and said, "The Salvation Army will be here by one to pick up the furniture and clothing."

If Truman didn't want to see it, that was on him. Thulani put all the photos in the box, except the one of the schoolgirls. He placed that picture on top of the box lid.

"These should go to someone," he told Truman.

Truman shrugged.

"Dunleavy wrote to someone from home."

Truman said, "No one claimed his body. I doubt if they will claim these tings."

Thulani expected as much from his brother. He combed through the garbage heap to find a bunch of letters that had been thrown into the pile earlier. He sorted through what envelopes he could find, setting aside two with recent postmark dates. He would pack up the pictures, minus the schoolyard photo, and send them off to the person who had written to Mr. Dunleavy last.

Truman tossed a kidney-shaped chestnut brown leather case onto the heap. Thulani had to investigate.

"You're supposed to bag this junk, not play with it."

Just as Truman could turn Thulani off, Thulani could do the same to Truman. He unbuckled the leather case. The letters *ED* were embossed in its leather above the huge brass buckle. Edmund Dunleavy.

Inside the case were a camera and a lens. It was a thirty-five millimeter, but not like the new ones he had seen in stores. This one was encased in metal, not plastic, and the lens was separate from the camera. He attached the lens, then raised the camera to the light to look through the viewfinder.

"It's junk," Truman said. "It doesn't work."

Nonetheless Thulani set the camera aside with the box of photographs, the letters, and the schoolyard photo.

It continued to rain throughout the week. Thulani's birds did not care much for the April rain, but he liked it just fine. The rain cleared the air when he ran through the park or stood on his roof. It made the fruit in the market smell strong. It was raining, but not hard, when he saw her among the green mangoes. Actually he saw her skirt first. Multicolored stars, planets, and comets against a black background.

Mr. Moon sighed. *Yeeeh.*

Thulani made his way to the mangoes, where she waited for him. He knew this because she did not avert her eyes as he approached.

"Hey," he said.

"Hello."

He was stuck for something to say and could only look at her.

She said, "Don't look at me like you miss me. You don't miss me. You have a girlfriend the next day. I know."

He blushed. "You—"

"Oh, yeh, I see you. And her. I said, 'Good for him.'"

"Is that what you said?"

"And I said, 'Let him worry her to death.'"

A woman shoved a bunch of grapes at him. He weighed them and handed the bunch to the woman without really looking at her. Mr. Moon grunted.

"I'm sorry if I worried you to death," he told her

sarcastically. "I only cared about you. Wanted to be your friend."

"Friend. Ha."

"You invited me into your house."

"It was late. Cold. What, I'm rude? You think I'd say, 'Go home, boy, in the cold?'"

"Oh," he said. "It was cold and you were polite. You weren't glad to see me."

"What you want me to say? 'Yes, Tulani, I'm so happy you came to my house with flowers'?"

"Was that so hard?"

"Look, I didn't want to like you. But there you are with your flowers. Tiny, little flowers with no smell. I don't want to like no one that way. You don't understand. I have things to do. I'm trying to graduate early. Get into a top design school. Boyfriends don't care about that. They want girlfriends to do this. Be here. Don't do that. They say, 'My girlfriend doesn't wear this. My girlfriend wear what I tell her.'"

He also remembered that night in her home. Seeing her sketches of the carnival dancer's body. A barely clothed body that was Ysa's, glistening in gold, red, and blue. For a second he saw her body, nude and bleeding. For more than a second he wanted her even when he should not.

"That sketch . . . it showed too much," he said. "I

didn't want to share you with no one."

"Ha. I didn't want to share my sketch with you," she said. "I covered it. But no. You have to see everything. Know everything. Then when I show you, what do you say? 'It is dirty. You are dirty. Hide, Ysa. Shame.'"

"Maybe I wasn't ready," Thulani said.

"Maybe *I* wasn't ready," she said back. "But you want, want, want." He was about to protest, but she cut him off. "No, you don't touch me, but I can feel you want, want, want. I said to myself, 'He doesn't even see what you can do. How does he know who you are?'"

"Ysa, I was pushing you. I'm sorry for that. I should have known you'd be afraid."

"Afraid? Me?" She became loud. "I'm not afraid of nothing. If it's something I want, I'm not afraid." She lowered her voice but spoke passionately. "I want to apply to college, so I had to take a complete physical with AIDS test and everything. You think I'm afraid? I fear no one. Nothing."

Mr. Moon reminded Thulani he had customers. Thulani ignored him, though he could not answer her. She was right. He wanted her but did not know her.

When it was apparent that he had nothing to say, Ysa took her items and stood on line while the other women in the market stared at her. She put her mango, four green plantains, two green peppers, and thyme on the counter for Mr. Moon to ring up. Then she left.

Mr. Moon said, "Forget about girlfriend. Too much trouble. Make you late for work or leave work early." He shook his finger at Thulani and warned, "Girlfriend get you fired."

When Thulani closed down the store and pushed the carts inside, he saw her standing across the street with her bag of produce. She had been waiting for nearly an hour. He crossed the street and told himself not to fall. Not to drink her in. Not to want her. Not to smile. Not to walk too fast as he crossed the street.

When he reached her, she said, "You're not going to walk me home?"

They started down the block toward Franklin. In the middle of the block she said, "You can take my hand, but you let go when I say let go."

He could do this. He could let go. He said, "All right," and took her hand.

FIFTEEN

Ysa caught him aiming the camera lens at her and gave him a severe look. These looks did not work on him as they once had. He could see the smile underneath her supposed annoyance.

"One more," he promised. "Just one."

"You take too many already," she said.

To both Ysa's and Mr. Moon's discomfort, Thulani used nearly a roll of film taking their pictures. He also took pictures of the produce and caught shoppers poring over yams, melons, and nectarines.

Since he had rescued the camera from the junk pile, he couldn't put it down. He spent many hours taking it apart to study the insides. Instead of going to class he sat in the library and perused books and magazines to learn about lighting, shutter speeds, and framing shots. The camera was not junk, as Truman had pronounced it. In fact Mr. Dunleavy had kept it in good condition. It simply had not been in use. Now that the camera was his, Thulani was rarely without it. He began on his rooftop, in the little time he spent there, waiting for his birds to fly off or return, trying to capture them in flight against the Brooklyn backdrop. In the house he took pictures of Shakira and followed his crawling niece, who seemed to enjoy being a subject.

Next he brought the camera to the market and tried to photograph Mr. Moon, who greeted Thulani's aim with his head down and arms up. Ysa was a bit more willing to pose, particularly if she wore one of her own designs. He liked to photograph her, regardless of what she wore. It was through the lens that he learned about her, such as how she could be completely serious about performing a task as small as comparing strawberries.

He hurried to frame her—the fruit in her hands and the street in the background—before the sun set. She appeared to be listening as he went on about what new thing he had learned about the flash. As he focused the lens, he could see that her expression clearly changed. Her two brows arched into one. Her jaw tightened. *What was it?* He put the camera down. The little strawberry baskets fell from her hands as she pushed past him and stormed down the narrow aisle to get at a woman at the yam bin. Ysa stood not more than two feet from the woman's face and screamed, "How does it feel to know you are the mother of a rapist?"

The astonished woman looked at her. Everyone did. Ysa was not deterred.

Thulani came up behind her, hoping to calm her. "Ysa . . ."

She put her hand up. *Leave me.* To the woman she said, "How does it feel to know you raise an animal? A dog? A piece of shit?" The woman tried to walk away, but Ysa stayed on her. "When you cook yam, do you know you feed the belly of a rapist?"

Mr. Moon implored Thulani to pull Ysa away. Thulani touched her shoulder, but she threw his hand off.

The woman was now angry. She said, "Little girl, you be careful how you speak to me."

Ysa hollered to the gathering crowd, "Look at her! Look at her face. Get a good look. If you see another face like it, it's the rapist's. Run. Hide your daughter."

"You want them to see something? I'll show them something," the rapist's mother bellowed, and at that moment Thulani could see that the woman had tolerated Ysa up until now and was not to be trifled with. She set down the bag of yellow yams and slapped Ysa across the face. Hard.

Ysa stood with her feet turned out to anchor herself. *You can't hurt me.* Waving her arms about, she shouted, "That's right. Mother of animal. Mother of dog shit. You don't make a human being. You make an animal. You make what you are."

The woman raised her arm to take another swing, but Thulani pulled Ysa away. He had to struggle. Ysa, who was all arms and legs, swung and kicked in every direction. With one wild swing she knocked his camera, still around his neck, against a pillar that stood in the aisle. He heard the cracking of glass but couldn't think of that. He had to get Ysa out of the store.

"Take her outside! Take her outside!" Mr. Moon said. To the rapist's mother he said, "No want trouble! No more trouble. Out! Go!"

Thulani led Ysa away from the rapist's mother and from the people who had gathered for the spectacle. He had felt this before. The people watching and their mouths moving as he and Ysa walked down the street. He had felt this that first awful night that he struggled to bring Ysa home. Not that any of these people cared about "that girl." They simply wanted to keep their mouths moving.

They walked past her house on Franklin. He couldn't bring her to Tant Rosie as hysterical as she was. Instead he brought her to the park, where she ranted in Creole and English, sometimes to him, sometimes to God. He just let her talk and talk while they sat on a bench.

"You see? You see? They grow up with mother. They grow up with father. Someone to say, 'Go to church, wash your face, study hard. Don't start trouble. Don't steal.' But they're dirty. They knock me down. Beat me. Rape. *Vyole.* They take everything from me. Everything." Finally she pushed herself into his chest and began to cry.

"Not everything," he whispered into her hair.

"You don't know," she sobbed. "You want to know, but you can't."

He knew she was right. He only wanted to comfort her. She dried her eyes on his T-shirt and began to rock herself in his arms. She said, "Before, I like everything about me. I like the sun shining on me. On my colors. I feel free. Open. Good like you are supposed to feel. But they take that. They take that from me."

He shook his head. "No, Ysa," he said. "You always have colors."

"Why? Because I kill a rainbow?"

She meant to make him laugh, but he didn't. He just held her.

"Stop being nice to me. I break your camera."

"I'll fix it."

She shook her head no. "I wouldn't let you touch my

portfolio because your hands were greasy, and I break your camera. You should be angry. Go ahead. Curse me."

"Stop it," he said. She looked up at him, a little surprised. He said, "Stop pushing me away. You think it's safer to be alone." He should know. He did everything to keep Truman and Shakira out.

He wanted to make her feel better, but all he could do was let her cry. When he was sure she was finished, he unzipped the camera case and took out the black-and-white photo of the three schoolgirls. He had planned to share it with her earlier, before everything went crazy. He looked up at the park lights and said, "It's not dark yet. I hope you can see this."

She wiped her eyes. "This photograph is old," she said. Her voice was husky from sniffling. "This is in your country?"

"Jamaica," he said, then wiped her eyes with his T-shirt. "Look close. What do you see?" He pointed to the schoolgirl in the middle.

"Your sister? No. Your mother?"

He nodded.

She smiled. "She is you."

"I look like my father too," he said with pride. "He's in Jamaica."

"And your mother's here in Brooklyn?"

He shook his head. "She died when I was thirteen."

She was silent, then finally said, "So sorry, my Tulani."

Rather than dwell on her simple declaration that he was hers, he said, "Why? Did you do it?"

She laughed a little but was still sad.

He did not think he could tell another soul about losing his mother, but this was no longer true. Ysa was not another soul but was becoming a part of his, even more than before, when he had thought of her every minute. Now all he wanted was to open himself to her.

"I wrote these letters almost every day when she went to Jamaica," he said. "My older brother knew she was going home to die, but I didn't. I mean, I knew she was sick, but I thought she'd get better. I begged her every day, 'I want to come. I want to see Daddy. Let me come. Why can't I come?' Every day, ten times a day. Can you imagine?

"I haven't seen my father since I was three. My father wouldn't come when we left for Brooklyn. I know he's in St. Catherine, but I wouldn't know where to begin looking for him. I barely remember him.

"My mother I remember. Games we played when I was little. Her voice, when it was stern or cheery. I know her recipes. She stood over me and taught them all to me that last year." He smiled, recalling to himself a particular cooking lesson. Oxtails. "I remember her giving my sister-in-law my baby clothes; I was mad. And her telling my brother to take care of the house. You know, as much as I pestered her, I can't tell you her last words to me."

Ysa said, "You still have a father."

"Somewhere."

Ysa kissed his face and his closed eyelids. She moved down on the bench, put his head in her lap, and gently rubbed his temples. "My Tuli, Tuli, Tuli. You try to know everything about me, so I tell you nothing, even if you guess right. So now I will tell you."

She traced the outline of his face with her fingertips and played with his hair as his dream girl had done on his rooftop. Except Ysa was not a dream. She would not run away.

When she was ready, she said, "A man left his wife and child in Haiti to come here for work. The wife is young. She grows lonely for her husband, so she packs her few things, puts her baby in her arms, and sets out to catch the ferry to Florida. That is where her husband is working. Florida.

"There is much confusion in Haiti. Unrest. Everybody wants to leave the island. The people come and come to take the ferry, but there are too many people. The ones who own the boat see this, but they don't care. They just want the money. God sees everything. He says, 'I'll show you greedy!' and in one breath the ferry tip over—and so close to Florida!

"Everywhere the people are drowning. Packages, people, floating in the water. There is screaming, shouting, crying. It is chaos. There are helicopters in the sky and boats everywhere. The coast guards shine lights all over, but they don't see everyone. It is night. Pitch-black. There are people in the water. Some swim to the boats. Some try to swim to shore. Some drown.

"A woman is calling out for her husband, 'Anton! Anton!' but he does not come to her. She asks and asks, *"Eske ou te wè Anton?"* but no one has seen the old man. It is crazy. People are just trying to save themselves and their things. In all the craziness someone puts a parcel in the woman's arms. She thinks it is clothes, but it is me. All night long she holds me tight in her arms and cries out, 'The ocean has my husband. Anton, Anton, Anton.'"

Thulani and Ysa shared the silence on the park bench as if they could see the scene before them. His thoughts whirling from her story, Thulani broke the silence and asked, "You never saw your mother?"

"Yes," she said right away. "Many times, when I was a baby. Tant Rosie overheard my mother tell another woman, 'My husband found work in Florida. He sent us money to come.' That is all she knows about my mother and father. Each year, she says, "Ah, Ysa. You look like the woman standing on the ferry, with your nose turned up and your eyes staring like so.' I know that is just for me, so I can pretend I know what my mother looks like."

But this was not all that she did not know. She did not know her true name. Her parents' names. The date of her birth. Anything.

At least he knew something of himself. He had thirteen years with his mother. Her recipes. Her stories. He had a picture of his father in his mind and the sound of his work boots. The songs he sang. Memories.

Ysa began to hum a melody, sad and slow. He felt the vibration of it through her body as his head lay in her lap. It did not seem right that she should cradle him. He lifted his head from her lap and sat up to hold her. She fell into the curve of his body.

She told him, "That was my lullaby when I was little and scared. She always sang that to me, my tant Rosie. 'The ocean has my husband. Anton, Anton, Anton.'" She looked up at him and said, "Sing that to me."

"What if you fall asleep?" he whispered into her hair.

"You will be here with me." She settled into his chest and said again, "Sing that to me, and I won't be scared."

And he did.

SIXTEEN

Thulani left his camera on his dresser and went to the fruit stand to see if he still had a job, especially after leaving Mr. Moon to close the store alone. As he expected, Mr. Moon gave him a hard time and turned his back as Thulani tried to explain Ysa's behavior.

"Too much trouble," Mr. Moon said. "Girlfriend bring too much trouble."

"She couldn't help it," Thulani said. "She saw the mother of the guy who . . . raped her."

"You not *stop* her," Mr. Moon accused.

"I couldn't," Thulani answered, knowing Mr. Moon would not understand. Ysa had to face that woman. It would have been wrong to stop her.

"I lose customers," Mr. Moon insisted.

Thulani implored Mr. Moon to look around him. There were plenty of customers in the aisles.

"I don't want trouble," Mr. Moon said, shaking his head and waving his hands. "No fruit, no Moon. No fruit, no Moon." This was what picketers chanted when they marched outside his store three years ago.

Thulani thought of Mr. Dunleavy, although Mr. Dunleavy would never have stolen. Stealing was beneath his needs and dignity. It was that Mr. Dunleavy was the only elder Thulani knew besides Mr. Moon. He easily placed Mr. Dunleavy's face on that of the old man who had taken the plums. He couldn't understand why Mr. Moon, a man well into his sixties, did not have pity.

"He was old," Thulani said.

"He stole my plums," Mr. Moon fired back.

"He was hungry."

"He stole."

"He was an old man. It was hot, and he was hungry."

Mr. Moon slapped his palm flat on a melon hide. "*My* plums! My plums. Thief!"

"That woman's son stole from Ysa," Thulani said without raising his voice. "More than plums. I know you understand me, old man."

Mr. Moon did not want to hear it, let alone understand anything about it. He tried to move away, but a customer stood in his path holding a watermelon that needed to be weighed. Mr. Moon threw up his hands and pointed to Thulani. "He weigh."

Thulani worked hard to make up for last night. In the evening he broke down all the wooden crates, tied up the cardboard boxes, pushed the carts inside, and hosed down the sidewalk alone. Then he went home.

Thulani let himself into the house. First he would go straight up to his birds and check on them, then he would wash up and eat. He had stopped counting his birds for some time now. They always returned and nested in the dovecote until the next morning. And if one did not return, what could he do?

As he entered the front room, he heard a strange voice say, ". . . once I tear down these walls, we can get the ball rolling."

Thulani couldn't move. He got an eyeful of the man who had spoken. He was a strapping, broad-shouldered man in his fifties with peppered hair and huge rings on his chubby fingers. Truman did not introduce them when Thulani entered the room. Nevertheless the man nodded to Thulani as he was quickly ushered out into the foyer.

Thulani sought out Shakira.

"Who's that? What's he talking about, tearing down walls?"

Shakira, nervous, said, "Talk to Truman."

"I'm talking to you."

For the first time since he had known her, Shakira was deliberately evasive. Uncomfortable. She got up and said Eula needed her.

Thulani cornered her. "It's seven-thirty. Eula's asleep."

"Talk to Truman" was all she would say. She wouldn't even look him in the face.

The man drove off, and Truman returned.

"It's done," Truman said. "The house is sold."

"You can't sell Mommy's house," Thulani said.

Truman was disgusted. "D'year that? Grown man talking Mommy. The house is sold. I told you we had plans. Not everyone sits on the roof watching opportunity go by."

"You can't sell the house," Thulani argued. "Half is mine."

"The house was left in my name. It is mine to sell."

"Mommy said take care of the house, not tear down the walls."

"I do as I see fit."

This was getting him nowhere. Truman had already made up his mind. The house was sold.

"Then give me the money Mommy left me."

Truman turned to Shakira. "Hear him? Give me, like he's a man." To Thulani he said, "We need that money."

"No," Shakira spoke up. "It's Thulani's. We'll have more than enough from the sale alone."

Truman turned to her and said, "Woman, this is between brothers."

Thulani said, "I need the money to live."

"You'll live with us in Jersey. Finish school. Work."

"I'm not living under you," Thulani said. "Once we close these doors, I go my own way."

"You have to come," Shakira said. "Where will you go?"

Truman said, "There's no other family to stay with. Where a go? Jamaica? You don't even know your father. You might as well don't have a father."

"You took this house, Truman. You can't take my father."

"No? Who raise you? Daddy?" He laughed. "Our mother said come, he won't come. She died, he won't come. What father? This is your father," he said, beating his own chest. "I am a man before I'm a boy."

Shakira stood between them. "Stop this. Stop this now," she pleaded.

"It's ended," Truman said. "The house is sold. We'll be out the end of June."

Just like that, the house was sold from under him. The walls of his mother's home would be torn down. He would be uprooted from his home as if he were a child with no voice. Although he had no place to go, he knew he would not live with them. As Truman said, he was a man. Why should he want to eat food he didn't work for and be reminded of it? He said to Truman, "Just give me what is mine."

To that Truman answered, "Our mother left college money. You don't make grades for college."

Thulani could not sleep. Truman and Shakira fought. Eula cried. The walls of his mother's home were being torn down, and his father was too far away. His bed seemed too small for his body. He rolled from one side to another but couldn't escape the stink of tobacco from the man's cigarette. He tossed and turned and seethed, for he realized Truman had let that man into his room.

He went to the rooftop with his camera to take pictures. When he stepped out onto the roof, he saw the big man pouring tar over the shingles. The dovecote had been smashed to pieces, but the birds were not inside. He looked overhead and saw Bruno leading the birds in as he always had. Thulani waved frantically and shouted, "No! No!" but could not stop them from landing on the rooftop. He ran out onto the thick, sticky tar in his bare feet and put his arms out for his birds to perch on. Instead of flocking to his outstretched arms, they descended onto the tar. All of them.

Like his birds, Thulani's feet also stuck fast to the tar. He watched, helpless, as his birds struggled, lifting their wings violently to break free. They pulled and fought until they all succeeded, leaving their pink feet in the tar. Some flew beyond the building; some flew just beyond the alley. At least three made it as far as the park. But one by one Bruno, Tai-Chi, Yoli, Dija, Esme, and the others dropped out of the sky. All he could do was watch.

Thulani woke up gasping. He was still in his bed. Ysa's skirt still hung before him. His photo of his mother and father stood on his nightstand. His camera was on the dresser, and the box of old photographs sat next to the camera.

Thulani fell asleep. When he awoke in the morning, he took a hammer up to the roof. He opened the door and released his birds as he had done every morning for three years. He followed them with his eyes as far as he could, and when he lost sight of them, he raised the hammer and swung and swung until the dovecote lay in pieces on the tar.

SEVENTEEN

"It's Saturday, Thulani. You don't have to be to work until three. Come see the house with us," Shakira coaxed.

Thulani shook his head no.

Shakira put Eula in his arms and said, "It has a big yard, front and back. I haven't seen it, but Truman says—" His glare stopped the words in her mouth. Truman was not a name he wanted to hear.

Eula took a handful of her uncle's dreads and put them in her mouth. Lately she put everything into her mouth, which amused Thulani, but he was still too angry at his brother to be distracted by his niece.

He said to Shakira, "You could have told me."

"It wasn't my place."

"That never stopped you before."

"I tried to tell you before, Thulani. Study. Have goals. Have a plan. Stick with school. Apply yourself for college. You don't hear me."

"By the end of next month I'll be homeless. Without money. That's not what my mother wanted."

"Whya so stubborn, Thulani? Come out to Jersey with us. At least see the house."

He knew Shakira wanted to keep everyone under one roof, one family. Still, he couldn't give in. He wasn't a part of the decision that would change his life. Only Eula should have her life dictated to her. No matter how much Shakira tried to convince him, he would not budge. He was no longer a child, as Truman had pointed out at the hospital. He'd have to find his own way.

He untangled his hair from his niece's grip and handed her back to Shakira.

"I gotta go."

He went straight to Ysa's house and rang the buzzer. His life was falling apart, and he needed to be with her. To rest his head in her lap, or hear her say things in her way. He simply needed to know there was still something good and solid in the world and that he could touch it.

She swung the door open and leaped into his arms

with the energy of a child. "I have news!" she said. "I can graduate next month!" She turned into the apartment and shouted in Creole to Tant Rosie, probably "I'm going out," then closed the door behind her. She took his hand and led him down the block in the direction of the park. He had never seen her so excited, as bright as the colors she wore. She did not stop talking.

"I've already applied to Parsons and FIT and Purchase and Pratt. And there's a school in San Francisco! Oh! And my counselor says my grades are so good I will get financial aid. I am set!"

He made himself say, "I'm happy for you, Ysa. You deserve it," although he felt her leaving him, sliding away from him just when he had a grasp on her. It made his stomach sick.

Ysa was too excited to notice. She grabbed his hand and said, "You're the first one I tell. Not even Tant Rosie knows."

He could barely look at her. He said, "I knew you'd graduate early. Get into a good school."

"I'm not in yet. I've just been sending applications, hoping I would graduate."

"They'll want you," he assured her. "You worked hard. You're talented. They'll want you."

"I feel good!" she said. "Happy."

He forced a smile for her sake.

They found the bench that was now *their* bench and sat down. She said, "You never came by so early. What is wrong?"

How could he cry to her when she was so happy? Look at her, he thought. Graduating from high school a year early, getting scholarships. A future before her. What do you have? What can you give her?

"Nothing," he answered.

"Ha! I know you. There is something wrong." He wouldn't look her in the eyes, so she took him by the chin. "Tell me."

"I destroyed the dovecote," he said. "The house for my birds. I took a hammer and smashed it."

"Why?" she asked.

"I couldn't sleep," he said. "I dreamed I tried to save my birds. Instead I killed them."

She did not understand, and he could not explain. He only knew it was wrong to possess birds.

"Why would you dream such a bad dream?" she asked.

"I can't help what I dream," he said defensively.

"Tulani, something is wrong." Her voice was no longer playful, no longer excited. "Something is making you feel bad inside."

He shook his head no.

"Tell me. I can take it," she said, but he wouldn't

budge. She became wild-eyed and said, "Your girlfriend. She sees us together and wants you back?"

Her jealousy stunned him so much he was slow to answer.

She pushed him with both hands. "Or you want her back? Is that it?"

He grabbed her before she could begin a tirade. "*You're* my girlfriend."

"That's what you better say."

He squeezed her tightly, and she delighted in being possessed. But still, he wasn't all right. Holding her worked only for the moment. He relaxed his embrace and sank his face in his hands.

"What is it? Why do you feel so bad? You have to tell me."

"My brother," he said, uncovering his face. "He sold my mother's house. He told me he'd sell it in two years, but I came home last night, and the house is sold. We have to be out by the end of June."

"My Tuli, my Tuli" was all she could say.

"It's my mother's house. When I'm in the kitchen, I remember her standing there. Or when I'm in the hallway, I see her at the linen closet." He threw up his hands. "The new owner can't tear down the walls fast enough." He swore he wouldn't cry, but anger filled his eyes with tears that rolled down his face. He turned away from her.

“Let me in,” she said softly. “Don’t push me away.”

That was what he had told her the other night. She leaned against him and said, “Oh, Tulani. Your home. I’m so sor—”

He took her hand. He didn’t want her to say that. He just wanted to be with her and let her back in.

“I’ll never meet your mother,” she said. “Will you show me her house?”

No one was home when he opened the door. He wanted to show off his fat little niece and for Shakira to say, “Madda Eula would have liked her.” Even so, he was glad that they had gone out to New Jersey. Truman was not fit to breathe in the same space Ysa occupied, let alone cast an eye upon her.

He showed Ysa the living room. The pictures of his parents. The curtains his mother made. Everything he could think of but his bedroom and the rooftop. When he destroyed the dovecote, he knew he would not return.

For Ysa everything was “nice” or “pretty.” It was as if she heard nothing, although her eyes never left him. He suspected she was nervous about being alone with him, but he would put her at ease. He had been with a girl before. He didn’t have to rush her.

Then he led her up the stairs to see his bedroom. He

was about to open the door when it hit him: Her skirt was spread out and nailed to the wall. He felt his heart flickering. He would lose her without a doubt.

"Ysa . . ."

She said, "I'm not afraid."

"No. It's not that," he said cautiously. "If I open the door . . . promise me you won't run."

"I'm here with you. Why would I run?"

He looked at her a last time. Once he opened the door she would scream. Run. First his mother's house would be gone. Then Ysa. He'd have nothing, nothing, nothing.

"Let me first—"

"No," she said. "Whatever it is . . ." She stepped inside. At first she saw only his bed, his dresser, the box and camera. Then she saw her skirt.

"I'll take it down."

"Leave it," she said firmly. Then again, this time calmly: "Leave it."

"We can go downstairs."

"We can stay here."

She removed her sandals and sat on his bed. "Come," she said. "Let's be here while we can."

He took off his sneakers and sat beside her. He felt nothing but shame as the skirt faced them. She tugged at him to lie down, but he couldn't. Not yet. He had to explain.

"That was all I had of you when I didn't know you but thought of you every day. Or when I'd find you and you'd disappear. Or when you made me mad." At this she smiled. "I never let anyone in my room because I didn't want anyone to see it, touch it, or ask me about it." He paused, hoping she would forgive him. "I'll have to take it down soon."

She lay down on the bed and pulled him on top of her. "We won't think about that."

This was all he wanted. To lie with her and kiss her and feel her and smell her and possess her. He needed only to be with her, squeeze her until they were one body. But Ysa was restless. Her hips spoke this restlessness. Finally she asked, "Tulani, do you have . . . protection?"

He nodded.

Didn't he want this? More than anything? Wasn't this what he burned for night after night? Somehow, even wanting her so much, all he could think of to say was "I'll hurt you, Ysa."

"I've *been* hurt, Tulani. You won't do that to me."

"No, Ysa. Feel me," he said, placing her hand on his penis. "I *will* hurt you, and I can't do that."

She took his hand and slid it inside her pants against her lips. "You feel? You see? I want you too."

He knew what it felt like to enter a girl and to thrust once he was inside inside. He didn't know what it would be like for her and why he didn't care with Julie. And now, as she urged him, her face willing and fearful, he removed his clothes. He said, "If you want to, you have to do it."

He lay on his back with his knees up. "I'm here," he said. "But you have to do it."

"Don't move . . . ," she said.

"I won't."

". . . until I'm ready."

She lifted her leg over his hips and knelt over him.

"Just be still," she said. "Stay."

"We don't have t—"

"Shh, shh. Stay. I come down slow."

"I'm here," he said. "I'm here."

She began to descend, her hands reaching for his. As she made her way down, half an inch at a time, it was all he could do not to move. He was flooded with her and the colors she carried in her. Now in him.

When she met him fully, he watched her eyes open and close in what he knew was pain, and what he prayed was the flush of vibrant colors. Behind her hung a sea of indigo and one hundred gold and turquoise eyes that would not blink.

EIGHTEEN

"Are you all right?"

They had been sitting on their park bench waiting until the sun went down, which was when he usually brought her home.

She laughed at him. "You asked me that yesterday, the day before, and the day before that."

He still worried. He could not help thinking he had brought back the pain inflicted on her almost a year ago in the alley. While she smiled and assured him otherwise, he could not believe her completely. Even so, he also knew he would not undo any of it. If he never felt another thing in his life, he had felt Ysa, and that was not to be taken back.

He said, "I have to make sure you're all right. You're my girl."

"Look at me, Tulani," she said, her eyes shining bright under the park lights. "I am smiling even when I am not."

"Okay." he gave in. "Then kiss me here"— he pointed to his lips—"and here"—to one eyelid—"here"—the other eyelid—"then we'll go."

Then he kissed her as she did him but resisted the urge to give her one last squeeze before they started toward her house. He took her hand and remembered what she once asked of him: to let go when it was time to let go.

Thulani came in quietly and lifted the lids on pots on the stove to see what Shakira had cooked for supper. He made himself a small plate of oxtails and vegetables and sat down to eat. He chewed around the bone and said to himself, I'll show her Mommy's recipe before they go.

Thinking of the move only reminded him he had no plan. The contentment he felt from being with Ysa faded.

"Good, you're here," Shakira said. Her voice was excited.

Truman followed behind her. From his expression, the exasperation of having been cut off in mid-speech,

Thulani knew they had been arguing.

"Here he sits," Truman said. Thulani filled in the rest, which was "eating my food."

"Eat!" Shakira ordered Thulani. "Eat everything. There is more in the refrigerator."

"What did I walk into?" Thulani asked.

"I'll tell you, braa," Shakira said. "Eula and I are not going to Jersey. We're going to Lincoln Place." Lincoln Place was where her parents lived.

Thulani put his fork down.

"Eat! It is *our* food. Not his," she said, pointing to Truman, "not mine, not yours. Our food. Eat well, because I'm packing up me and Eula to go home."

"Shakira, stop your drama. You're my wife, and my wife and daughter comes with me."

Shakira said, "Give Thulani his money. Then your wife and your daughter come with you."

"You're messing with tings not your business," Truman warned, but Shakira did not seem to care, or change her stance.

"Not my business? What? Truman d'na marry *I and I*. Truman marry Shakira. True?"

Thulani nodded. True.

"One flesh, one blood, true?" she asked her husband. "*Cha!* How can I sit in my house and enjoy my washing machine, my flower garden, when I know

Thulani roam the streets with no home? You think that makes me happy? You think I can have peace? Raise my daughter to be decent when we steal from her uncle?"

"Thulani has a place with us. This is how I planned it."

"But this is not what Madda Eula wanted. I sat with her, Truman. These are not her wishes, and I'm not a thief. I canna *live* in a house not mine."

Truman turned to Thulani. "You see you cause? I try to keep the family together, you split everyone t'hell apart."

When he came home the next evening, Thulani found a bankbook on the table. It was in both his and his mother's names. He opened it. The deposits had begun the year he was three and ended the year he was thirteen. The interest had added up through the years. He closed the bankbook and put it in his wallet.

"You have to make your way on that, Thulani," Shakira said. "And y'beddanot make me out a fool. Y'hear me?"

He hugged his sister-in-law and promised he wouldn't disappoint her. By the same token, as he hugged her, a world of things occurred to him, now that he had means.

NINETEEN

"I will be gone a month," he told Mr. Moon.

"No job when you come back," Mr. Moon replied.

"How can you be like that, Mr. Moon? I have to see my father in Jamaica."

"No come, no job."

In spite of the finality in Mr. Moon's tone, Thulani was not worried. He could get his job back if he had to. It just wouldn't be easy.

He lifted his newly repaired camera to take a picture of Mr. Moon. As usual Mr. Moon quickly put his hands up.

Ysa, on the other hand, posed for many pictures in her graduation dress, which she had designed herself. She had chosen a bright white fabric that picked up colors when hit by the sunlight. Iridescent, she called it.

He took pictures of her in her cap and gown standing with a camera-shy Tant Rosie. He managed to get one close-up of her face at the moment that her hand touched the fake diploma.

Ysa was anxious to have photographs taken of the dress. Once the ceremony was over, she removed her blue robe and cap and gave them to Tant Rosie to bring home, while she and Thulani went to the park. There Thulani tried to capture Ysa in her dress as the sun set off its many colors.

He promised to bring her copies of the photos when he returned from his trip.

"No, no. Mail them to me," she insisted. "I want to look forward to receiving them."

"I'll be back soon," he promised, but she did not seem satisfied. Her eyes were sad. She said, "I wish we could be together one more time, like we were."

He kissed her on her lips and on her closed eyelids as she had always done for him. "I'll be back soon," he said.

They sat on their bench. She said, "Tulani, I want to tell you something, but I don't want you to be upset."

What?

"I felt pain."

"Ysa." He squeezed her hands, but she pulled back.

"No, no. Not how you think. I mean, I felt what we

did. That we were together."

He took her hands again, gently. She said, "I want us to be together one more time, so after you fly away, I will still feel us together. Inside."

He tried to laugh at her, but she was serious. "I'll be back before you miss me," he promised. "I just need to see my father. You'll see."

"Tulani, that's what you say. But you will see the place you were born. Your father. How rich the land. You'll be home. I know."

"I'll be back before—"

"Ssh, ssh," she said. "Let's sit here and not speak." After a while she said, "You can sing me my lullaby." And he did.

Shakira gave Thulani the addresses of her relatives and directions to his father's house. Eula gave her uncle a drooly kiss. Truman had already given him the bank-book, and that was all that he would give.

Truman and Shakira had already begun packing for their new home. Thulani wanted to leave before the house was stripped of everything his mother put in it. He did not want to be there when they left. He had to be the first to go.

He packed neatly. His clothes and possessions all went into one large duffel bag. He would carry the box of photographs and the camera with him on the plane.

He looked back at his bed, the dresser, the nightstand, and finally the walls. He had to let go of everything. Everything except the skirt, which he saved for last to pack. He removed each nail carefully so as not to tear the fabric. This took some care, as he had driven the nails deep into the wall. The silklike fabric fell into his arms with ease when he released the last nail. He laid Ysa's skirt out on his bed and folded it in half, fourths, then eighths, turning the gold and turquoise on the wrong side. Even so, he could still see her eyes before him, opening and closing, opening and closing, opening and closing. . . .